Custardfinger

The lorry had pulled up to the kitchen door and stopped. It was a red lorry with a sort of yellow splash painted on the side and the single word SCOFFCO. The driver's door opened and out hopped two burly figures in bovver boots and gingham frocks. Buster recognized them at once: they were Pansy and Petunia. Miss Burtle and Poppy hurried with them into the canteen. Buster crouched beside one of the scraggy little trees that stood at the front of the school and watched as they began to carry big crates out of the kitchen and load them aboard the lorry.

"Weird!" he whispered.

"You're right, lad," said the tree. "Now get off my foot!"

Look out for more books in this series:

Night of the Living Veg
The Big Freeze
Day of the Hamster

PHILIP REEVE

Buster Bayliss

Custardfinger

**Illustrated by
Graham Philpot**

■ SCHOLASTIC

Scholastic Children's Books,
Commonwealth House, 1-19 New Oxford Street,
London, WC1A 1NU, UK
a division of Scholastic Ltd
London ~ New York ~ Toronto ~ Sydney ~ Auckland
Mexico City ~ New Delhi ~ Hong Kong ~ Smogley

First published by Scholastic Ltd, 2003

ISBN 0 439 98090 9

Typeset by Falcon Oast Graphic Art Ltd.
Printed and bound by Nørhaven Paperback A/S, Denmark

10 9 8 7 6 5 4 3 2 1

1
TUBA TROUBLE

"And now," said Mr Fossilthwaite, the headmaster of Crisp Street Middle School, "we're going to round off this morning's assembly with a very special treat."

"Hmmfffgfffhmmf!" spluttered Buster Bayliss.

"Z////////," said all the other pupils and teachers, slumped in their uncomfortable plastic seats.

It's quite difficult to send people to sleep when they're being made to sit on bum-numbing chairs which were probably designed as instruments of torture for a medieval dungeon (and then turned down by the torturers for being too cruel) but Mr Fossilthwaite always seemed to manage it. At nine o'clock each Monday morning the whole school would troop into the hall and sit down. At one minute past nine they were all still wiggling about trying to get comfortable. By two minutes past, heads were nodding, eyelids were drooping, open mouths were dripping dribble on to school jumpers and even the teachers were starting to yawn.

Today, they were all in for a rude awakening.

"As you know," the headmaster burbled on, "Thursday night is Parents' Evening, and we very much hope that all your mums and dads will be coming along to have a look round the school and find out a bit about what you've all been getting up to this term. . ." (He hesitated for a moment, as if it had just occurred to him that most of the mums and dads would be better off not knowing.) "Er. . . As a way of showing them some of the work of the school," he went on, "I'm afraid there will be a special performance by our very own School Orchestra!"

"Zzzzzzzzz . . . whassat?" said his audience, waking up and looking at one another in alarm. "Did he say School Orchestra?"

"Gnnnfffffhmmfhehehehh," went Buster, quivering with poorly muffled laughter near the back of the hall.

"The orchestra have been working very hard

this term," Mr Fossilthwaite burbled, "and they've learned a brand new piece of music to play on Parents' Evening. We're very . . . er . . . privileged to be able to finish our assembly with a special sneak preview. . ." (He quickly fumbled in the pocket of his tweed jacket for some earplugs.) "Let's have a big round of applause for Miss Taylor and the School Orchestra, who are going to play us Wolfram Von Agasplatt's Tuba Concerto in G Flat!"

"Aaaaaaaaaargh!" whimpered all the children, wide awake by now, and a few of the more highly strung teachers looked as if they might make a break for the exits. The School Orchestra wasn't something you wanted to hear early on a Monday morning. Or late on a Monday morning. Or on any other morning or afternoon or evening ever.

Try imagining a herd of angry woolly mammoths emptying a skip-load of old tin baths off the top of a multi-storey car park. Noisy, isn't it? But compared with the sound the Crisp Street School Orchestra made, it's a soothing little lullaby.

For the poor pupils and teachers packed into the school hall that morning, there was no escape. The curtains behind Mr Fossilthwaite swooshed open to reveal Miss Taylor, the music teacher, beaming happily as she raised her baton to begin the concert. On three rows of seats at the back of the stage the School Orchestra crouched, ready to begin the torture; hammers were poised over glockenspiels, fingers curled over the air-holes of recorders and right in the middle of the front row Buster's fake cousin Polly Hodge took a deep breath and put her lips to the mouth-piece of her enormous tuba.

"Oh nooooooo!" whispered the orchestra's victims, clamping their hands over their ears or wrapping jumpers round their heads.

"Hmfgfhahaha!" Buster cackled wickedly. He knew what was going to happen next.

Polly's mum, Fake Auntie Pauline, was Buster's mum's best friend, and when they went round to her house for tea the day before she had insisted on telling them all about how well Polly's tuba lessons were going, and playing them a CD of Agasplatt's Tuba Concerto. It started off with a tinkle on the glockenspiel, followed by a long, lingering toot on the tuba. That was what Buster was waiting for. Unlike everyone around him, he was looking forward to it.

Miss Taylor waved her baton.

Tinkle, went the glockenspiel.

Polly puffed into the tuba with all her might. Her round face turned pink, then red, then purple with the effort.

No sound came out at all.

The rest of the orchestra watched her worriedly, but everyone else in the hall looked quite relieved. Maybe this was going to be one of those modern bits of music which are just made up of silence! Even the School Orchestra couldn't get one of *those* out of tune.*

"Fgggnnnnnnnnnurrffff!" spluttered Buster, enjoying every minute.

"Hurrrrrnnnnffffffffffffffffff!" went Polly, blowing harder than she'd ever blown in her life.

And suddenly the tuba belched out a great strangulated raspberry and the hall filled with snow. Up out of the instrument's round brass bell came a blustering blizzard of whirling white, blotting out the stage completely and then swirling out across the front rows of the audience, white flakes doing dizzy little dances in the glow of the neon lights.

Miss Taylor screamed, the orchestra gasped, and everyone else cheered, realizing the concert would have to be cancelled. A few people sneezed, too, because as the snowstorm started to settle it turned out not to be snow at all, but

*Well, not too badly. . .

5

feathers; hundreds and hundreds and hundreds of little white feathers.

As for Buster, he just cackled.

Up on the stage, Polly threw down her tuba and stormed off, and the rest of the orchestra went with her. Miss Taylor glared down angrily at the sea of happy, feather-speckled faces in the hall. She didn't know who was responsible for this feather-related outrage, but she could guess. It was probably the same person who had got jam on her xylophones. The same person who had accidentally sat on her second-best violin. The same person who had once tried to tunnel his way out of her room in the middle of a music lesson.

"Buster Bayliss!"

Near the back of the hall, Buster did his not-very-good best to stop sniggering and look innocent. "What?" he asked.

* * *

It wasn't really Buster's fault. The temptation had just been too great to resist. If you'd been at your fake auntie's house for tea, and had just been made to sit through a whole CD of Wolfram Von Agasplatt's Tuba Concerto, you'd probably have felt like a bit of light relief too. And if you'd happened to notice that your fake auntie had left a big old goose-down quilt folded up on top of the wheelie bin for the dustmen to take it away, wouldn't it have put ideas into your head?

Buster had left Polly and the grown-ups talking and slipped out into the hall, where Polly's tuba waited, ready for the next morning's assembly. He took it out of its case and dragged it into the front garden where the wheelie bin stood, and then carefully scooped as many handfuls of feathers as he could from inside the quilt and packed them down into the tuba's innards, squidging them in tightly so that they didn't show and wouldn't come out until Polly blew really hard.

Of course, quite a lot of feathers escaped during the process, and when Fake Auntie Pauline came to wave Buster and his mum off at the front door a little later the garden looked like Santa's grotto, but she hadn't guessed that Buster was to blame. "Vandals!" she said crossly. "Quilt-ripping hooligans! I don't know what the neighbourhood is coming to!"

"Or maybe it was a fox," said Buster's mum.

"Gnrffffherherher!" said Buster.

Unfortunately, he couldn't really explain all that to a grown-up, so when he was dragged into the headmaster's office after assembly and Mr Fossilthwaite asked him why he had played such a silly practical joke he just looked down at his trainers and mumbled, "Don't know."

"Oh well," said Mr Fossilthwaite happily, "that's all right then. No harm done, eh? Now, don't do it again. Off you go!" He was just as relieved as everybody else that he hadn't had to sit through Agasplatt's Tuba Concerto, and he had secretly been wondering about giving this intelligent young Bayliss some sort of medal.

Unfortunately, Miss Taylor was also in the office (it was she who had dragged Buster there, using his left ear as a handle). She was still very angry at having the orchestra's performance ruined, and she wasn't prepared to see the Phantom Tuba Stuffer of Crisp Street let off so lightly. "Just a minute, Headmaster!" she cried, grabbing Buster by his other ear as he headed for the door and swinging him round to face Mr Fossilthwaite again. "Surely you're not going to let this little barbarian get off without some sort of punishment?"

Mr Fossilthwaite looked nervously at the music teacher. He wondered if he should tell her that there were still rather a lot of feathers clinging to her hair and clothes, but decided it might not be a good idea. "What did you have in mind?"

"I thought we could have him torn apart by wild horses?"

"I don't think that's allowed, Miss Taylor. Anyway, we haven't *got* any wild horses."

"Oh. Well then, what about tying him up in a sack and throwing him into the River Smog?"

"Again, Miss Taylor, not strictly allowed. The Parent Teachers Association tends to frown on that sort of thing, you know."

"Really?" Miss Taylor frowned, dislodging a feather that had been stuck to her right eyebrow. "Honestly, no wonder children these days are so ill-behaved! Whatever happened to good old-fashioned discipline? Still, I insist you do something to punish this miscreant."

"Er . . . detention?" suggested Mr Fossilthwaite amiably.

"Pah!" cried the music teacher. "This is Buster Bayliss! He laughs in the face of detention! What we need is a punishment so excruciating that Buster will never, ever, ever want to pull a trick like this again!"

Mr Fossilthwaite thought about suggesting that Buster should sit in on all the School Orchestra rehearsals till the end of term, but then thought better of it.

"Um, such as?" he asked.

Miss Taylor leaned close to Buster, and there was an evil gleam behind her glasses as she prepared to reveal her fearful revenge. "Make him work on the school magazine!" she snarled.

Buster looked at Mr Fossilthwaite. Mr Fossilthwaite looked back at Buster. If they had been cartoon characters there would have been little clouds full of question marks above their heads.

"*What* school magazine?" they asked.

"*The* school magazine!" shouted Miss Taylor. "You know, *Crisp Street Confidential*. It comes out once a month. Miss Brown's the teacher in charge, but Polly Hodge is the editor. She spends half her lunchtimes working on it, and frankly it's a waste of good tuba-practising time. What she needs is a little helper. A little helper like *Buster!*"

Mr Fossilthwaite looked uncertain. This sounded more like a punishment for Miss Brown and Polly than for Buster. But that gleam was back behind Miss Taylor's glasses, and if there was one thing he had learned in all his years of headmastering it was Never Argue With An Angry Music Teacher. "Very well," he said. "Buster, you'll report to Miss Brown's room as soon as you've had your lunch."

"But, but, but, but, but!" stuttered Buster. "But that's in lunch hour! I've got important things to do in the playground! People to see! Games to play! Ben and Tundi have challenged 3a to a game of Busterball and I'm their star striker!"

Miss Taylor smiled coldly. "Well," she gloated, "you should have thought of that before you started packing feathers into other people's tubas, shouldn't you? Hmmmmmmmffffggggnffff-hhahahahahahah!"

2
CRISP STREET CONFIDENTIAL

That lunchtime, Buster woofed his packed lunch down as quickly as he could and hurried off to Miss Brown's room. Well, maybe "hurried" isn't quite the right word. Maybe "trudged" is more like it. Trudged very, very reluctantly, grumbling all the way about how (grumble grumble) unfair it was, being made to go and work on the (grumble grumble) school magazine when everybody else was doing nice lunchtimey things. He could hear the excited shouts of his friends playing Busterball out in the playground as he knocked on Miss Brown's door. He knocked very quietly, in the hope that she wouldn't hear, but she did, and called, "Come in!"

Buster poked his head around the door.

Miss Brown was one of the nicest teachers at Crisp Street, and Buster secretly thought she was very pretty. She was a very tall lady with a round smiley face at the top, and her ears were rather big and poked out through her long, brown hair like two pink satellite dishes (so no wonder she'd heard his knock). She was quite funny, and almost never told him off when she was on playground duty, and all in all Buster felt that if the school was ever attacked by Zurgoid Destructor Cyborgs or washed away in a freak flood, Miss Brown was probably the person he would rescue. That should have made spending a lunch hour in her room quite a nice thing to do, but unfortunately Buster always got a bit flustered when Miss Brown smiled at him, and being flustered made him embarrassed, and pretty soon he was just a little red, bumbling bundle of bashfulness.

"Hello, Buster!" said Miss Brown, smiling.

"Mnnf!" said Buster, bashfully.

"Gosh, why have you gone that funny colour? Are you all right? Come in and take a seat. . ."

Rather reluctantly, Buster slithered his way into the room. It had that abandoned, echoey, *Marie Celeste* feeling that classrooms always get in the lunch hour, even though it wasn't completely empty. At a desk in the front row sat a large pair of glasses with a small boy behind them, and next to him sat Fake Cousin Polly, who almost fell off her chair when she saw Buster. "Aaargh!" she screamed. "What's *he* doing here?"

"Sorry, Polly," Miss Brown laughed. "I should have told you. Mr Fossilthwaite's sent Buster to help us with the magazine. Ooh, now *you've* gone a funny colour. Should I open a window or something?"

Polly hadn't just gone a funny colour*; she was shaking all over. She looked as if steam might start hissing out of her ears at any moment. She'd sometimes been quite glad of Buster's help in the past (mainly when she was being menaced by hungry sprouts or turned into a garden ornament by wicked witches) and she had to admit he was quite good at fighting off ice-monsters and luring giant socks into cunning traps, but she didn't see what use he could be to her school magazine. Anyway, she hadn't forgiven him yet for what had happened that morning. "He'll just ruin everything!" she complained. "He's a hooligan! He's a juvenile delinquent! He's... He's the sort of person who fills people's tubas with feathers!"

"It was only a joke," protested Buster, who hadn't reckoned on Polly being quite this upset.

A rather fetching purple with a hint of maroon.

15

"*Tuba Terror Strikes Crisp Street!*" said the boy beside her, scribbling notes on a fat, spiral-bound jotting pad as he spoke. "*Hundreds Feathered in Symphony Sabotage! 'It Was Only a Joke,' Claims Twisted Feather-Brain Bayliss. . .*"

"Neville likes to talk in headlines," whispered Miss Brown. "It gets very wearing. . ."

Buster took a good look at this Neville. Not only was he wearing huge glasses that made his eyes look three sizes too big for his head, he also wore a battered old trilby hat with a label attached to it. Buster peered at the label. "PRESS", it said. He pressed it.

"Oi!" said Neville.

"See?" wailed Polly. "He's already going around pressing people's hats! He's a one-boy crime wave!"

"But it says PRESS," Buster pointed out.

"Yes," said the boy, straightening the hat, "but it doesn't mean PRESS as in PRESS. It means PRESS as in journalist. I'm Neville Spooner, fearless boy reporter." He held out an inky hand, which Buster shook. "I'm *Crisp Street Confidential*'s top writer," he went on. "Well, actually, I'm its *only* writer. In fact, apart from Miss Brown and Polly, I'm its only reader."

"I'm not surprised," muttered Buster, leafing

through the heap of back issues on Miss Brown's desk. Now that he saw the little photocopied four-page magazines he realized that he had noticed them lying around the school before, gathered in dusty heaps on window sills and the tops of cupboards. They looked so dull that he'd never bothered to find out what they were.

A Life With Mops said the front page of one. *We interview Crisp Street Cleaner Elsie Mangle about her forty years of service to the school!*

Exclusive! blared another. *New Hopscotch Grid Planned for Playground! Full details: pages 2,3 & 4.*

"Miss Brown!" pleaded Polly. "You can't let him help! It'll be an absolute catastrophe!"

"Well, I think we should give Buster a chance to prove what he can do," said Miss Brown, smiley as ever. "You must admit, Polly, that if you're to get the latest issue out before the end of term, you'll need some extra help. And we haven't exactly got people queuing up to write for us. . ."

Polly glared so hard at Buster that it was a wonder her glasses didn't melt. "All right," she said. "He can write one story."

Buster perked up a bit. He quite liked writing stories. Maybe this punishment wouldn't be so bad after all. "Can I do one about vampire alien zombies that eat people's brains?"

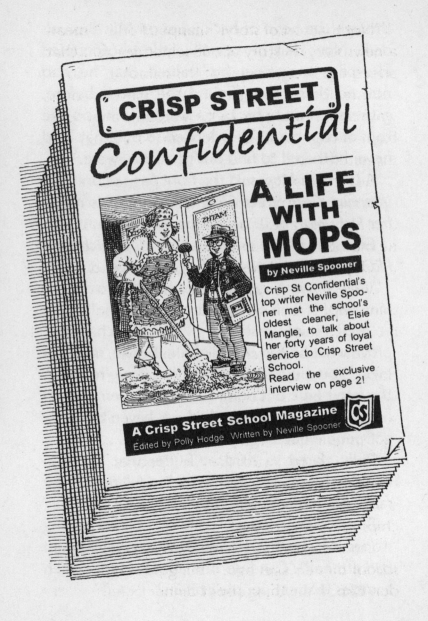

"Not that sort of story!" snapped Polly. "I mean a news story! A story about something real that affects the lives of pupils at this school."

Buster looked thoughtful. "Well, maybe I could write about how Miss Taylor is actually a vampire brain-eating zombie alien in disguise," he suggested.

"But that's not true!"

"It might be! You don't know for sure that she's not! She's got a really mean streak. She wanted to tie me up in a sack and throw me in the river."

"Oh, if only!" sighed Polly, going all wistful.

"Well, I bet it would get more readers than some soppy exclusive about a hopscotch grid," grumbled Buster.

"Now, now, Buster," said Miss Brown. "Polly is the editor of our magazine, and that means that it's up to her to decide what goes in it. What would you like Buster to write about, Polly?"

"Dinner ladies," said Polly.

"That's good," said Neville Spooner. "Strong human interest stuff; *The Truth Behind the Apron – My Life With a Ladle*. The ups, the downs, the chips . . . I like it, chief."

"Dinner ladies?" said Buster. "But I gave up having school dinners ages ago. I bring packed lunch. I don't know anything about dinner ladies!"

"Well, go and find out tomorrow lunchtime then," said Polly. "The school canteen changed hands at the beginning of this term. It's been handed over to some private company to run, and I want to tell everyone how they're doing. Bring me a five-hundred-word article about it by Wednesday morning break: what the new menu's like, whether it's healthy, is private catering good for Crisp Street, all that sort of thing."

"Awwwwhhh," said Buster, feeling as if he'd just been given triple geography homework.

Polly leaned closer to him, and spoke softly so that Miss Brown couldn't hear. "And if you do it really, really well, and don't muck about, and don't pretend the new dinner ladies are brain-eating alien zombies in disguise or serving minced-up first years in their curry or something, there's just a small chance that your mum will never get to hear about the feather thing."

"Gulp!" said Buster, and he meant it. As usual when he had a Brilliant Idea, he hadn't stopped to think how his mum would react. What on earth was she going to say when she found out about this morning's tuba-blizzard? With Polly's mum being Mum's best friend, it would be all too easy for his fake cousin to let her know what had happened. Mum would probably stop his pocket money for so long that he'd be about fifty before he had enough to buy another Mars bar!

"So, is that all sorted?" asked Miss Brown cheerily.

Buster nodded. So did Polly. "I'll meet you at the canteen tomorrow, Buster," said Neville Spooner. "I'll take some snaps; you do the words. This could be the beginning of a beautiful friendship."

3
SHADY DINNER LADIES

The canteen at Crisp Street was a long, two-storey building wedged uncomfortably into a draughty corner of the playground. It looked as if it had been built out of Lego sometime in the 1950s. The walls were the colour of old chewing gum. Downstairs were the school kitchens, with steamed-up windows and a gaggle of big wheelie bins outside where failed meals were dumped. Upstairs was the actual canteen bit, full of peeling lino, formica tables and a smell of greasy chips. Buster hadn't been inside it for ages, because he'd complained so much to Mum about all the boiled beetroot, half-baked beans and stodgy pud he was being forced to eat that she let him start taking packed lunches instead.

The canteen was already packed with pupils by the time he climbed the stairs and pushed his way in through the doors, but he heard someone calling his name and looked round to see Neville Spooner waving at him from a nearby table. There was a camera and a jotting pad on the chair beside Neville's and when Buster came over he said, "I've saved a space for you. Go and get your dinner from the counter."

Buster picked his way between the tables to the counter, where three dinner ladies waited to serve him. He was surprised to see that they weren't the same ones he remembered from his last trip to the canteen. Then he noticed the big red and yellow sign hanging on the wall behind them. *This is a Scoffco canteen*, it said. He remembered what Polly had said about a new company taking over the running of Crisp Street's school dinners. They must have got rid of the old dinner ladies and brought in their own people. Buster wondered if the food would be any better.

The new dinner ladies were rather large and hairy, but they seemed friendly enough. The first had a name-badge saying "I'm Poppy" pinned to her frilly gingham uniform. She flashed Buster a smile full of gold teeth and said, "Chips, dearie?"

"Er. . ." said Buster, and a heap of soggy chips

splattered on to his plastic plate.

"And I can recommend the boiled beetroot," said Poppy, whose voice was surprisingly deep and gruff. Buster nodded. Poppy picked up her ladle, which was enormous and made out of that pale grey metal you only ever see in school kitchens, and used it to pile a purple mound of beetroot next to the chips. Buster put the plate on his tray and moved on.

The next dinner lady's name-badge said "I'm Pansy". She had a stubbly beard, and a tattoo of a skull on the top of her arm. "Whodjerwant, kid?" she asked. "A nice spam fritter, or the Vegetarian Option?"

"What's the Vegetarian Option?" asked Buster.

"String," said Pansy.

"Um, then I'll have the spam fritter, please," said Buster.

The last dinner lady was called Petunia. She had cauliflower ears and an eye-patch and she was serving the afters. "It's Bakewell tart today, mate," she announced, shovelling something dry and pale brown on to a plate and plonking it down on Buster's tray.

Buster looked down at his dinner and sighed, imagining the nice packed lunch he could have been eating, heavy on the crisps and chocolate biscuits. This canteen nosh looked even nastier than he'd feared. There wasn't even any custard! In the old days, the one good thing about school dinners was the canteen custard, which was very thick and incredibly yellow and tasted not quite like any other custard. A splodge of that would cheer up his rock-hard Bakewell tart no end.

"Got any custard?" he asked hopefully.

Petunia went white. Poppy dropped her ladle. Pansy clenched her fists and glared.

"Custard's off, dear," said the lady sitting at the cash-desk at the end of the counter. To Buster's surprise she was someone he knew: Crisp Street's old head dinner lady, Beryl Burtle. She had been as jolly and friendly as all the other dinner ladies in the old days, but today she seemed to be in a bad mood; she glared at him with her beady black eyes and said, "There's a national custard shortage, or haven't you heard?"

"Oh, is there?" said Buster. "All right then. I'll just have this lot."

"That'll be two pounds fifty," snapped Miss Burtle, holding out a plump hand for the money.

Buster paid up, but as he was turning away from the counter his eyes were drawn to the window behind Miss Burtle's seat, and met another pair of eyes staring in through the smeary glass. That seemed strange, what with the canteen being on the second floor and everything. Stranger still, the eyes belonged to Mr Creaber, Crisp Street's grumpy old caretaker. He gave a startled jerk when he saw Buster looking at him, and fell sideways out of sight. Buster thought he heard a scream and a distant crash, but he couldn't be sure, because of all the clatter and chatter of the other diners.

Grown-ups are weird, Buster thought, carefully steering his tray of gruesome grub back to where Neville was waiting.

"What's old Beryl Burtle doing here then?" he asked, sliding into the seat that the Ace Boy Reporter had saved for him and starting to scoff his chips. "I thought this place had been taken over by some private company?"

"It has," explained Neville. "It's Miss Burtle's company. She's the owner of Scoffco. She set it all up last term, and went to the council and said she could do school dinners for half what the old dinner ladies used to cost them, so they gave her the contract. She fired all the old staff and brought this new lot in. I think that was a rotten thing to do. The old dinner ladies were really nice; Doreen and Nesta and Mrs Crust. They were really friendly, and they always chatted and asked you how things were going, but not this new lot . . . I don't know . . . I can't quite put my finger on it, but there's something strange about them."

Buster looked at the dinner ladies. Pansy was scratching her beard and Petunia was cleaning her nails with what looked like a flick-knife. "Maybe it's a good angle for this story Polly's making me write," he said.

"You mean, *Fishy Goings-on in New Look Canteen?*" suggested Neville, in headlines. "*We Dish Up the Dirt on Dubious Dinner Ladies. . .*"

"Yeah!" said Buster, his brain beginning to buzz with exciting ideas. "Maybe they really *are* brain-eating space zombie aliens in disguise. . ." Then he sighed and shook his head. "No. I promised Polly I'd keep it real and relevant and all those other boring things. We'd better just do a story about how foul the food is."

Neville took a photo of his plate.

"I wish there was some custard," said Buster, prodding the top of his Bakewell tart with a fork.

"Crikey! Are you on afters already?" Neville looked in amazement at Buster's empty main-course plate and took a quick photo, muttering, "*Crisp Street Boy Scoffs School Nosh in Record Time!*"

"I liked the old school custard," Buster went on. "It was nice and yellowy and thick."

Neville took another photo, this time of the whole canteen. "There hasn't been any custard on the menu all term, now I come to think of it," he said. "There's a shortage, apparently. I think it's to do with the mystery custard factory explosions."

"Mystery custard factory explosions?" asked Buster, pressing down a bit harder on his Bakewell tart, which pinged off his plate and made a dent in the wall.

"Yeah," said Neville excitedly. "It was on the news. Custard factories all over the country have been suddenly exploding for no reason and. . ."

His voice trailed off, and Buster became aware of a presence looming over him in a loomy sort of way. He looked up, and saw that Beryl Burtle herself was standing beside the table, glaring down at Neville.

"And just what do you think you're doing?" she demanded, sounding hissy and dangerous and not at all like her old, friendly self.

"I was just taking some photos," explained Neville nervously.

"They're for the school magazine," Buster agreed. "We're doing an article about how nice all your food is."

"Snooping, eh?" Beryl Burtle reached out quickly and snatched Neville's camera, stuffing it into a pocket of her flowery apron. "No photographs are permitted in this canteen!" she told him.

"Hey!" Neville complained. "You can't do that! That's my sister's digital camera!"

"Well, I'm confiscating it," said Miss Burtle firmly. "You can have it back at the end of term."

"But. . ."

"Now, if you've finished your dinners, you'd better run along. Other people are waiting for seats, you know. . ."

"But. . ." said Neville, but Miss Burtle was already chivvying the two boys towards the exit. Glancing over his shoulder, Buster caught a quick glimpse of Poppy, Pansy and Petunia looking on with worried expressions.

"Well, what was all that about?" he said, when they were out in the playground again. "Why would she be so worried about somebody taking a few photographs?"

"How am I going to get my camera back?" said Neville. "That's the real question. I mean, it belongs to my big sister, and I sort of forgot to ask her before I borrowed it. If she finds out I've gone and got it kidnapped by dinner ladies she'll wreak some kind of hideous vengeance!"

Buster shrugged. Miss Burtle's strange behaviour had made all sorts of questions start scurrying around inside his mind, but he remembered his promise to Polly and carefully stamped on them. He felt sorry for Neville, of course – it was terrible to think that some people had to go through life lumbered with a big sister – but he didn't see how he could help. "Maybe she just won't notice?" he suggested hopefully. "It's only a couple more weeks to the end of term, and you'll be able to get the camera back then."

Neville let out a sort of hollow groan. "Oh, she'll notice. She's going to London with her boyfriend next weekend, and she's bound to want to take some pictures. I suppose it might make a story for the mag, though. *Tragic Death of Star Reporter – Rampaging Big Sister Feeds Crisp Street Boy to Pet Terrapin. . ."* He suddenly stamped his foot, making his hat slip down over his eyes. "It's not fair! I was only taking some snaps! I'm going to go back in there and demand that camera! Coming?"

"Sorry," said Buster, and hurried quickly away. He was in enough trouble already, without picking fights with dinner ladies. From the far side of the playground he watched as Neville strode back into the canteen. He felt a little twinge of guilt, wondering if he should go and back him up, but it quickly faded. Ben and Tundi ran past, shouting at him to come and play Busterball – they were losing to 3a by ten million goals and needed a touch of the Bayliss magic if they were to equalize by the end of the lunch hour.

Buster shook his head. "Just a minute, OK?" He had a deadline to meet. He sat down on the school steps, pulled out a scrumpled scrap of paper and a well-chewed pencil, and began to write.

* * *

"How was school?" asked Buster's mum when he got home that afternoon.

"Blahhhfarrgleblurrrb. . ." said Buster. It had been spelling and history all afternoon and he was so bored that he couldn't even talk. "Snurrble. Floob."

"That's nice!" said Mum cheerfully, not looking up from her newspaper.

"Flaahhh?" said Buster indignantly. "Flahplahflah-blah *flahhh!*"

"Mmmm," agreed Mum.

Buster put down his school-bag in a sarcastic manner. He was starting to get the idea that she wasn't listening. With a huge effort, he regained the power of speech. "What's for tea?"

"Fish and chips," said Mum. "I haven't thought about afters yet. Any requests?"

Buster had a quick think. "Any chance of some custard?" he asked, hoping to make up for his disappointingly custardless lunch.

Mum shook her head. "Sorry. There's a national custard shortage, apparently. I've just been reading about it. Look!" She held up the newspaper she had been reading so that Buster could see. The *Smogley Evening News* wasn't usually very exciting (it had only slightly more readers than *Crisp Street Confidential*) but today it had a startling headline splashed all across the front page in big black letters. *CUSTARD CRISIS!*

"It's terrible!" Buster's mum explained. "There was a huge explosion at the Bunchester Custard Factory in the early hours of this morning. Nobody was hurt, luckily, but the factory's been flattened and the whole neighbourhood has been splattered with scorched custard. It's the fifth custard factory that's blown up this week. The authorities are baffled. Look. . ."

She held up page two. It said, *AUTHORITIES BAFFLED!*

"So that's why there's no custard at school!" said Buster. He switched on the TV and hopped channels until he found the local news. Firemen were busy cleaning up the custard-slick in the streets of Bunchester, and a reporter was interviewing one of the eyewitnesses, who was saying, "Well, Trixie, I heard this big bang, and then there was a sort of blurbling noise and everything just went yellow. . ."

Back in the studio the newsreader put on his gloomiest voice and said, "So what's causing this spate of custard-factory catastrophes? At first, police suspected sabotage, but trendy TV chef Damon Crumble (presenter of *The Flying Chef*) today suggested a more sinister explanation. . ."

Damon Crumble appeared, wearing a T-shirt that said *Cookin' is KICKIN'!* Buster recognized him. He had a really lame programme where he flew all round the country in a helicopter and landed in people's gardens to cook meals for them. Like most TV chefs he had stupid hair, and didn't look that much older than Buster.

"Britain's custard-makers were recently forced to change their recipes to comply with new regulations, right?" Damon explained. "I think the new recipe has something to do with these explosions, right? For some reason, the mixture is unstable, and explodes when warmed. I don't want to sound, like, alarmist, right, but I believe all custard in Britain today is highly explosive!"

"Crikey!" said Buster's mum. "I'm glad I wasn't able to buy any now! I'd better phone up your Fake Auntie Pauline and warn her; she always keeps a few tins in her store-cupboard, and she's just had a new kitchen put in. If it gets splattered with exploding custard she'll be a *trifle* annoyed!"

"Auuugh!" groaned Buster, covering his ears with sofa cushions while Mum laughed at her own ghastly joke. But talk of Fake Auntie Pauline reminded him of Polly, and that reminded him that he had work to do. "Mum?" he asked. "Can I use the computer? I want to type something for the school magazine. . ."

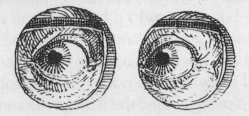

4
THE WHEELIE BIN OF SECRETS

At break the next morning, Buster went looking for his fake cousin. He found her among a little crowd of girls on the music-room steps, all talking about shoes and hair and last night's episode of *Lovely Doctors* and other things that no self-respecting boy should ever have to hear. Pushing his way through to Polly he tried to keep both ears covered while at the same time digging about in the loathsome depths of his rucksack for the story he had promised her.

"Finished!" he said, holding it out

Polly adjusted her glasses and peered at the piece of paper until, beneath all the creases, splotches, crossings-out and odd stains, she noticed some words. They said:

Our New Skool Canteen by me, Buster Bayliss, Class 2b

Our skool canteen is under new manugement so all the old dinner laides have been kicked out for being rubish except for one she is called Beryl Burtle and the canteen is run by her companny called Scoffco. The new diner laides are called Poppy, Pansy and Petuiana and they are verry nice but if you try to take photograps of them they tell you off and take your camrer off you which is really bad news specially if it is your big sisters camrer and she has got a boyfriend and keeps terrorpins. The food is still HORIBLE. I had some chips and some beetrot and some spam friter and I was going to have a Bakewell tart for my afters but it was a bit too well baked and it ESCAPED. There wasn't any custard because Nevile says it might EXPLOD, which would be a pitty. It cost £2.50p my Mum says it is daylight robery.

Polly turned the paper over, but there was nothing on the back except three squashed gnats and a drawing of a spaceship. "Is that it?" she asked.

Buster nodded. "I tried typing it all out neatly

on Mum's computer, but when I tried to check the spellings it went phut. It's good, isn't it? I've made it all relevant and serious and I haven't mentioned alien zombies once."

"I don't know what to say," muttered Polly, clinging on to one of her friends for support while she quickly read the report through again.

Buster thought for a moment. "How about, 'Well done, Buster, what a brilliant piece of reporting, you're my hero and there's no danger at all that your mum will find out about any alleged tuba-feathering incidents'?" he suggested. "That ought to cover it."

To his amazement, Polly just scrunched his brilliant report up into a tight little ball and threw it at him. It bounced off his nose. "Ow!" he said. "What did you do that for?"

Polly was turning the colour of canteen beetroot. "That," she said, pointing at the balled-up paper as it rolled towards a nearby drain, "is the worst news item that anybody has given me during all my weeks as editor of *Crisp Street Confidential*. Anyway, I asked you for five hundred words!"

"But I don't know that many!" protested Buster. He made a headlong dive to rescue his work, but missed by a millimetre, and watched in dismay as the squodge of paper rolled through the grating and dropped to a watery doom in the sewers. He wasn't going down *there* after it – the sewers of Smogley were usually full of goblins, aliens and rampaging monster socks, not to mention poo.

"Maybe you could just use the pictures instead?" he suggested. "Neville took some photos in the canteen yesterday. You could do a big splodge over two whole pages, like in a glossy magazine, with captions. . ."

Polly had been about to tell Buster off some more, but now she stopped. She hated to admit it, but sometimes he did have some good ideas. "Hmmm. A picture spread! We haven't done one of those before. A picture is supposed to be worth a thousand words – and that's just the usual sort of words, spelled right, so a picture's probably worth about nine zillion of your words. Where are these photos?"

"Er . . . you'd have to ask Neville," said Buster. "Miss Burtle took his camera away, but he went to get it back."

Polly's frown deepened until it measured 7.9 on the Bayliss Frown Scale. "Is that what all that rubbish about big sisters and terrapins meant?" she asked. "I didn't understand that bit."

"I 'speck he's got it back by now," said Buster. "I mean, Miss Burtle was just in a bad mood yesterday. She wouldn't really confiscate a camera, would she? Not from somebody who was wearing a hat that said PRESS on it. Come on, let's go and find him and ask him."

"Neville's not here," said Polly. "He wasn't in class this morning. He wasn't here yesterday afternoon, either. Miss Brown had a note from his mum to say that he'd had to go home at lunchtime."

"Argh!" groaned Buster. "But that means no photos! And *that* means. . ."

"That means you'll be spending your lunchtime in Miss Brown's room with me, writing that article out properly," said Polly, "using a dictionary and everything."

"But, but, but!" Buster objected. It was useless. As he stood there butting, the bell rang, and Polly and her friends began to drift towards the school as if a Zurgoid Graviton Beam was tugging them back to their desks. "See you at lunchtime, Buster!" Polly called.

Buster was immune to Zurgoid Graviton Beams and to school, so he didn't join the tide of children as they ran and trudged and hopped and shuffled back into their classrooms. Instead, he hid behind the bike sheds until the playground had emptied, then scurried towards the canteen. He had just had a Brilliant Idea. What if Miss Burtle *hadn't* let Neville have his camera back before he went home yesterday? That would mean that it was still sitting in her desk drawer, or her apron pocket, or her spare saucepan, or wherever it was that dinner ladies kept the things they confiscated. If Buster asked really, really politely she might let him have it, and he could take it to Polly at lunchtime and say, "Here are the snaps. No need for an article now, eh? I'm off to play Busterball! See you!"

The doors of the canteen were locked, but the windows of the kitchen on the ground floor were already steamed up and from inside came the clatter and clank of hundreds of helpings of dinner being prepared. Buster straightened his shirt collar, smoothed his hair, checked his nose for bogies and reached out to knock on the kitchen door, putting on his most angelic smile. But just before his knuckles touched the door's peely paintwork he overheard Miss Burtle's voice coming from inside. "Pansy!" it yelled. "Poppy! Petunia! I want you to keep a special eye out for snoopers this lunchtime! I don't want any more of those little creeps from the school magazine sniffing about!"

Buster jerked back his knocking hand just in time. It sounded to him as if Miss Burtle was still in a fierce mood, and something told him that even his cheesiest smile wasn't going to cheer her up.

"What about that one from yesterday?" asked a gruff voice – Pansy's, Buster thought.

"He's been taken care of," said Miss Burtle, and laughed a laugh so spine-chilling that Buster felt as though somebody had just dumped a scoop of ice cream on the back of his neck and it was slithering all the way down to his pants.

He scurried away from the door and round into the narrow alleyway between the side of the canteen and the playground wall. Leaning against one of the huge wheelie bins there, he tried to sort out all the scary ideas which were whizzing about inside his head. So Neville hadn't gone home at all! That note that Miss Brown had had from his mum must have been a fake! Buster had watched enough television to have a pretty good idea what had really happened to him: Miss Burtle and her dinner ladies really *were* alien brain-eating zombies. When Neville went back into the canteen to talk to them he must have seen something that proved it, like a big pile of fresh brain-burgers in the fridge. Miss Burtle must have done away with him so he couldn't write about it in the *Crisp Street Confidential*!

"Ulp!" said Buster. He wondered if he should run and tell a teacher about what he had just overheard – Miss Brown, perhaps. But Miss Brown was a grown-up, and grown-ups were all the same, even pretty ones with sticky-out ears – they never believed Buster, and they always fell for everything evil alien space-invaders told them. There was no point even telling Polly about this until he had some proof.

He crept gingerly to the nearest window and peered through. Unfortunately, it was so steamed up that he couldn't see anything. He was just about to try another window when a side door creaked open and Petunia stomped out, carrying two bulging black bin-bags.

Buster ducked into the shelter of the wheelie bins just in time. Crouching down, he peered between the wheels and saw Petunia's hairy legs and high-heeled shoes come closer, closer. There was a grunt as the dinner lady tipped her bin-bags into the bin, and then she turned and went back into the kitchens.

"Phew!" said Buster. He waited until Petunia was safely back inside, then scrambled up and perched on an abandoned crate so that he was high enough to open the lid of the bin and peer

inside. He was hoping (in a shivery sort of way) to find that Petunia had been throwing away a lot of left-over first years or a few stale brains, so that he could prove to everybody that the dinner ladies were up to no good. All he saw, spilling out of the burst-open bags, were a lot of potato-peelings and fish-heads.

And then, half buried in the smelly heap, he saw something that made his blood run cold. It was a crumpled trilby hat, with a label pinned to it marked PRESS.

"Gulp!" said Buster, leaning into the bin and pulling the hat out. As he closed the lid again he heard a faint movement behind him, and almost fell off his crate in his haste to turn round. There was no one there. At least, he couldn't see anybody... But in the side of the next-door wheelie bin two little holes had been bored, and for a moment he was almost sure he glimpsed two beady eyes staring out at him, before whoever it was ducked down out of sight.

For once, Buster decided that he would rather be inside the school than out in the playground. Clutching the hat, he tiptoed past the kitchen gate and then bolted towards the safety of his classroom, making up excuses as he went about why he was so late.

* * *

That lunchtime, Buster really did hurry to Miss Brown's classroom. Miss Brown was out on playground duty, but Polly was sensible enough to be allowed to stay there without supervision. She was sitting at her desk, an open book in front of her. Buster plonked Neville's hat down on it.

"What's that?" asked Polly, leaping backwards. "And why does it smell of fish?"

"It's proof!" said Buster dramatically. "Those new dinner ladies are up to something all right. That's Nev's hat; I found it in a wheelie bin outside the canteen."

"Oh yuck!" wailed Polly, fanning the air in front of her nose to keep the pong at bay. "Trust you to go hunting about in wheelie bins!"

"But Nev's been eaten!" said Buster.

"No, he hasn't, Buster."

"But the new dinner ladies are zombie aliens!"

"Stop being silly."

"I'm not being silly!" wailed Buster. "Don't you remember all the bother we had with those man-eating sprouts? Or that time Mum unleashed all those ancient forces of evil from under the school playing field? Things like that go on all the time in Smogley. And nothing weird has happened all term, so we're about due for another flare-up!" He wondered if he should tell her about the watcher in the wheelie bin, but decided not to – now that he was back in the safety of the school, he half thought he'd imagined those spying eyeballs. "If Nev hasn't been eaten," he said, "then where is he, that's what I'd like to know!"

"Spudsylvania," said Polly, with a smug smile.

"What?"

"I checked with Miss Brown. Apparently Neville's gone on holiday. He's visiting his cousin Eggbert in Spudsylvania."

"Then why are dinner ladies throwing his hat away?"

"Maybe he dropped it. Or left it in the canteen. . ."

"Why did Miss Burtle say he'd been taken care of?"

"Buster, that could have meant anything. She might have meant she'd taken care of him by giving him a good telling off. Or giving him back his camera and sending him away with a free canteen cookie. It doesn't mean she's eaten his brain! Who'd want to eat Neville's brain? It's only about the size of a Malteser, and it's stuffed full of stupid headlines."

That was a good point, but Buster still wasn't

convinced. He knew a Sinister Plot when he stumbled across one. "Beryl Burtle and her dinner ladies are impostors, I just know it. I bet if you pulled their hair-nets hard enough their heads would come off, and there'd be something yucky underneath, with tentacles. They're probably using those wheelie bins to hatch out their unearthly spawn."

"I don't think so, Buster," said Polly. She poked Neville's hat away with a ruler and showed him the pile of books she had been studying. They were old Crisp Street School year-books from forty years before. "While you've been wheelie-bin-diving, I've been doing some research for that article you're supposed to be writing. It turns out Beryl Burtle used to be a pupil at Crisp Street herself. Look. . ."

From the bottom of the pile she pulled out a long, thin photograph showing the whole school lined up in rows on the playing field. The face she pointed to, at the end of the back row, was unmistakably a young Beryl Burtle. "See? I bet she's got some wonderful stories about Crisp Street in the old days. It was the Sixties, you know; the era of Swingin' Smogley. I might try and do an interview with her for the magazine. Or get her to write her own column. . ."

"Why's she in twice?" asked Buster. He pointed to the other end of the row, and there was Beryl Burtle again, looking exactly the same except for a strange little smirky smile. "She's in two places at once! How'd she do that if she isn't some sort of weirdy extra-terrestrial being with amazing super-powers?"

"Oh, Buster," sighed Polly, "people always do that in these panoramic photos. They're taken by a special camera that moves round slowly, and if you're quick you can run from one end of the row to the other before it's finished taking the picture and get in twice. That's why Beryl looks so pleased with herself. Our mummies always appear twice in all their school photos. Haven't you noticed?"

Buster shrugged. His mum had shown him her school photos once, but all he remembered were rows and rows of dim-looking girls with hockey sticks and his mum saying, "Blah blah blah that's me drone burble blah and there's your fake auntie Pauline blah drone." He wished he'd paid more attention now. Then, as he stared at the photo in Polly's hands, he noticed a third face he thought he recognized. "Look! It's Mr Creaber!"

Polly gave a little gasp. "You're right! I'd never have recognized him with that Beatles haircut and those trendy shades! Well, I never knew *he* was an Old Crisp-Streetian. . ."

"Poor old Creaby!" said Buster. "Going to school in this dump is bad enough, but imagine getting stuck here being caretaker for the rest of your life, fixing the boiler and mopping up other people's sick. Maybe that explains why he's always so tetchy. . ."

But Polly wasn't listening. "Ooh," she said, "we could do an an interview! We could ask him all about how the school's altered since he used to be here, and the challenges of modern caretaking! Come on, let's go and talk to him now!"

"Now?" cried Buster, shocked. "It's lunchtime! You should never get between a caretaker and his lunch: I thought everybody knew that!"

"Oh, yes, I forgot." Polly looked thoughtful. "But, I can't go after school, because I've got tuba practice, and tomorrow lunchtime would be too late – that's when I have to photocopy the latest issue." She looked thoughtfully at Buster. "You'll have to do it."

"Me?"

"Tonight, after school."

"You mean, at going home time?"

"Yes. It won't take long. Just nip down to Mr

Creaber's office and ask him a few questions. If you write down the answers without too many spelling mistakes, I'll forget about the canteen article, and your mummy will never hear about the whole tuba thing."

"Gnnnngg!" said Buster, because it's frustrating having to obey your fake cousin just because of a bit of innocent tuba-tampering. But the more he thought about interviewing Mr Creaber, the more he found he sort of liked it. The school magazine would give him the perfect excuse to talk to the grumpy old caretaker. He wouldn't be asking about how the school had changed and the challenges of modern caretaking, though. If Creaby had been at school with Beryl Burtle, he might know her sinister secret. Maybe he would be able to help Buster find out what she and her so-called dinner ladies were really up to!

5
SKLONK – WAAOOOOH – SPLAT!

When the bell rang at the end of the afternoon Crisp Street School emptied in a cheering, yelling rush, with pupils flooding out of every exit like water out of a leaky bucket, only noisier and not so wet. The teachers were not far behind them, chugging away in tatty old cars with "I swerve to hit kids" bumper stickers and teetering piles of marking on the passenger seats. Soon, only the School Orchestra remained, lugging their instruments into Miss Taylor's music room to practice for Parents' Evening. Buster could hear them tuning up as he ran along the corridor to Mr Creaber's office.

Now that it was time to actually confront the caretaker, Buster could not help feeling a bit nervous. He and Mr Creaber had a love-hate relationship: Buster loved annoying Mr Creaber, and Mr Creaber hated Buster. They had never really seen eye to eye since Buster's first term, when he had altered the sign outside the main gate from *Crisp Street Middle School* to *Rice Crispy Street Muddle School*, and having to clear up all those feathers after Monday's assembly probably hadn't made the caretaker any more pro-Buster. But some of Polly and Neville's journalistic curiosity seemed to be rubbing off on the Bayliss Brain – Buster badly wanted to find out the truth about Beryl Burtle, and old Creaby seemed like the best person to ask.

He summoned up his courage, stuck a label saying PRESS on his shirt, and knocked on the caretaker's door. There was no answer. He tried again, and squashed his ear against the door to listen out for snoring. Nothing. It was very odd. Mr Creaber was nearly always in his office at this time of day. Buster knocked again, then mooched out into the playground.

He hung around for a while in full view of the office, flicking bits of grit at the window and waiting for the curmudgeonly caretaker to come running out and tell him to hop it. Mr Creaber did not appear, but a rattling sound came echoing eerily from somewhere at the front of the school. *So that's where he is*, thought Buster, hurrying towards the noise. It sounded as if he was locking the big front gates. But that couldn't be right – the School Orchestra were still practising. Mr Creaber wouldn't want to lock them in. *Out*, maybe, but not *in*. . .

Buster rounded the corner of the school, and saw that it wasn't Mr Creaber who was making the rattling noise. Miss Burtle and Poppy were busy pulling the gates open as wide as they would go so that a ginormous lorry could reverse in. BEEP, BEEP, BEEP, VEHICLE REVERSING! it said, over and over, as it backed into the playground and rolled towards the canteen. Buster thought that was really stupid, because lots more people must get run over by lorries when they were going forwards, but you never heard any that went BEEP, BEEP, BEEP, VEHICLE GOING IN THE RIGHT DIRECTION!, did you? He didn't have time to think much about it, however, because down at the canteen all sorts of interesting things were happening.

The lorry had pulled up to the kitchen door and stopped. It was a red lorry with a sort of yellow splash painted on the side and the single word SCOFFCO. The driver's door opened and out hopped two burly figures in bovver boots and gingham frocks. Buster recognized them at once: they were Pansy and Petunia. Miss Burtle and Poppy hurried with them into the canteen. Buster crouched beside one of the scraggy little trees that stood at the front of the school and watched as they began to carry big crates out of the kitchen and load them aboard the lorry.

"Weird!" he whispered.

"You're right, lad," said the tree. "Now get off my foot!"

"Yargh!" Buster tumbled backwards, but luckily Miss Burtle and her dinner ladies were too busy with their loading to notice him and a sudden blatt of noise from the music room drowned out his frightened howl. From a hole in the trunk of the fake tree, Mr Creaber's face scowled down at him.

"What are you doing sneaking about on school property after hours, Bayliss?" it asked.

"I'm being a daring boy reporter for the school magazine, Mr Creaber," quivered Buster. "That's why I've got this label on my jumper. I'm sorry I stood on your roots. I didn't know you were a master of disguise."

"I have to be, in this job," grumbled the old man. "Have to keep my eye on things, don't I?"

"You've been spying on the dinner ladies!" Buster realized. "That's what you were doing up that ladder at the canteen the other lunchtime. And those eyes in the wheelie bin – that was you!"

"Might have been," the caretaker admitted grumpily.

"They're up to something, aren't they?" Buster asked. "I think they're brain-eating alien zombies!"

"Rubbish!" said the caretaker. "Still, there's something going on, right enough. This lorry, for instance. It's been here every night this week. Miss Burtle told me it's delivering supplies for the kitchens, but there's another one that comes in the mornings to do that. This evening lorry isn't delivering anything. It's taking something away!"

They watched as Miss Burtle and her henchwomen loaded a few last boxes aboard and slammed the doors of the lorry shut. Petunia and Pansy climbed back into the cab and drove off, while Miss Burtle and Poppy went back into the canteen, shutting and bolting the door behind them.

"They never leave that place," said Creaber. "I've been watching, and I've never seen them go home. But they don't sleep in there either – I've shone my torch in through the windows after dark and there's nobody there, just an empty kitchen."

"Spooky!" said Buster. "So what do you reckon they're up to?"

Mr Creaber shrugged, showering Buster with badly painted paper leaves. "How should I know?"

"Well, you know Beryl Burtle, don't you? You were at school here with her. I saw your photo. Polly reckons your hair made you look like a beetle, but I thought it looked quite good."

Mr Creaber's beady eyes looked Buster up and down. "All right, Bayliss," he said, "let's talk. But not here. In my office. . ."

* * *

In Mr Creaber's office, everything was the colour of tea: a spare tea-coloured coat hung on a tea-coloured hook on the tea-coloured wall, and some unhappy-looking tea-coloured pot-plants struggled to survive on the tea-coloured window sill, stretching their dry leaves up into the light that filtered down through the dusty, tea-coloured glass.

"Cup of tea?" asked Mr Creaber, shrugging off his tree costume and boiling some water in a tea-coloured kettle.

"No thanks," said Buster, who was more of a fizzy orange person.

The caretaker shrugged and filled his tea-coloured mug with some tea-coloured tea, topping it up with milk from a tea-coloured fridge. *At least if he spills it it won't show*, thought Buster.

Mr Creaber settled himself into a creaky brown armchair and slurped his tea. "Now," he said, "how much do you know about this canteen business?"

Buster shrugged. "Only what I already told you. Miss Burtle wouldn't let us take photographs, and now Neville's gone missing. Mrs Brown had a letter from his mum to say he's in Spudsylvania, but if that's true, why's his hat in the canteen wheelie bin? That Miss Burtle's a brain-eating zombie for sure!"

Mr Creaber frowned so hard that his eyebrows tangled together, like two Brillo pads having a fight. "For the last time, Beryl Burtle isn't a zombie," he said. "She's my girlfriend!"

"Oops," said Buster.

"At least," the caretaker continued, "she was. We were childhood sweethearts, see, when we were nippers here back in the old days. But Beryl was brighter than me; top marks in Home

Economics every week. She got a scholarship to an elite dinner-lady training college down south. Pigbin's Academy of Canteen Catering, it's called. All the top dinner ladies are trained there. She spent years perfecting her baked bean stirring and her mashed-potato dolloping. They taught her special meditation techniques, honing her mind to razor sharpness until she could plan a whole term's menu in under a minute. She had to do cross-country runs in full dinner-lady kit, pushing fifty helpings of fish and chips on a heated hostess trolley – toughening her up, see, so that she'd be able to lug all those great heavy pots and pans about. She passed her final exams with flying colours. When she left, they awarded her the Golden Ladle. She could have got a job in any school canteen in the country; she had her pick. But she chose to come back here to Crisp Street. Me and her have been walking out together ever since. . ."

Buster stifled a yawn. He had been expecting shocking revelations about gruesome goings-on in the canteen, and instead he was listening to a load of old rubbish about dinner-lady school and Mr Creaber's love-life! He was so bored that he couldn't keep his eyes open or his mouth shut, and he was just about to keel over and have a nice snooze in Mr Creaber's mop-bucket when the caretaker said, "But she's changed!"

"Changed how?" asked Buster, mustering just enough interest to open one eye.

Mr Creaber shook his head in despair. "It's just this past term, since she started her own company: this Scoffco thing. She's got no time for me any more. All she's interested in now is making money. It's not just our canteen she's in charge of now, you know; Scoffco do the dinners at St Collander's Middle School, and Nigel Kneale Community College, and that old people's home on the Bunchester Road. The weird thing is, they don't even cook food on the premises any more: they just buy it all in and heat it up. That's not like Beryl at all. She always loved cooking! And listen to this. . ."

He suddenly dropped to his knees, and pressed his ear to the tea-coloured lino on the office floor. Buster copied him. Faintly, from somewhere below, he heard a strange noise: Zoosh zoosh zoosh zoosh it went. Grundle-grundlegrundle. Ghurrrrrrr.

"What's that? The school boiler?"

Mr Creaber shook his head, which isn't easy with one ear pressed to the floor. "I've been tending that boiler for forty years, I know every little sound it makes. This is something new. Started a few months back."

"Something to do with the dinner ladies?" asked Buster.

Mr Creaber sat up stiffly. "I just don't understand it!" he said. "Beryl's never been the sort to get involved in mischief. Even as a girl, she was always the best behaved pupil at Crisp Street. Nice, sensible lass, a bit like that Polly Hodge."

"She popped up twice in the school photo, though," Buster pointed out.

"Eh?"

"The school photo. Polly showed me. Beryl ran round and got in twice, so she must have been a *bit* naughty. . ."

"Oh, but that wasn't Beryl!" said Mr Creaber. He went to his desk and moved aside a basket full of confiscated balls and catapults to reveal his own copy of the old school photo. It had faded to the same tea-colour as the wall behind it, and there were some dead flies trapped inside the frame, but the faces of those long-ago Crisp Streetians were still visible. "That's Beryl," said Mr Creaber, pointing to the girl on the left of the back row. "That one on the right is her sister, Myrtle."

"But they're identical!" gasped Buster.

"No, not really," said Mr Creaber. "Not really alike at all. Look at Myrtle's nasty, sneery expression. She was a bad 'un, that Myrtle. Forever off playing truant and getting into scrapes. A good cook, mind, like her sister, but a nasty nature. She went to Pigbin's too, but she got herself expelled for her wild ways and daringly avant-garde potato-peeling techniques. I wonder whatever happened to her after that? Beryl never talks about her, but. . ." His eyebrows suddenly shot upwards like the roofs of two exploding custard factories. "Flamin' 'eck! You don't think it could be *her*, do you? What if Myrtle's done away with Beryl somehow and taken her place?"

"But why?" asked Buster.

"To get her hands on my school!" growled Mr Creaber. "I should have thought of that before!" He made his way over to a tea-coloured locker in a corner of his office, and fumbled through his big bunch of keys for the one that would open it. "I've been neglecting my duties, Bayliss. It's a caretaker's job to take care of his school, and I've let that Myrtle Burtle start hatching her nefarious plots right under my nose! Who knows what she's done with my poor little Beryl? And who knows what she's up to in that canteen? Probably stealing school property and shipping it off the premises in that Scoffco lorry!"

"Maybe we should call the police?" suggested Buster.

"No, lad." Mr Creaber flung the locker door open and lifted out a broom. Somehow Buster could tell that it was very old, but its head was clean and bushy and its long handle had been polished so highly that it seemed to shine with a brownish light. Mr Creaber's face shone, too, as he held it up in front of him. "This was my father's broom," he said softly. "My dad was caretaker here before me, and he handed this on to me when I took over. 'You look after this place, Albert,' that's what he told me. 'There's all sorts of evils can befall a school: graffiti, vandalism, burst pipes, break-ins, supply teachers. . . It's your sacred duty as a caretaker to protect it. . .'" He made a few experimental swipes with the broom. They were quite impressive swipes, but Buster still felt worried.

"What are you going to do, Mr Creaber?"

"I'm going to nip down to that canteen, lad," said the caretaker. "And I'm going sort out those new dinner ladies once and for all!"

He slammed out of the office, and Buster hurried after him, a bit nervous, but eager to see what happened when an unstoppable caretaker met an irresistible dinner lady. Through the silent corridors of the school they went, past walls of artwork put up ready for the Parents' Evening tomorrow, past the school hall where the half-decorated stage awaited the School Orchestra's performance of Agasplatt's Tuba Concerto, past 1b's big colourful collage of the water-cycle with its silver-foil oceans and cotton-wool clouds. The late sunlight slanting across the rooftops struck bright highlights from the handle of Mr Creaber's broom as he unlocked the back door and started across the playground towards the canteen. As he went he rummaged among the keys on his key ring, and by the time he reached the kitchen door he had the right one in his hand, ready to slide into the lock.

Except it didn't fit.

"They've changed the locks!" he gasped. "But *I'm* the only one authorized to change locks around here! Of all the—"

"Oh well, better go home then," said Buster, who was secretly quite pleased, because the closer he had got to the canteen the more he found he didn't want to confront Beryl Burtle, or Myrtle Burtle, or whoever she was. "Maybe we should just try again tomorrow. . ."

"No!" Mr Creaber's fighting spirit had been aroused, and he wasn't ready to give up so easily. "There's nothing else for it. We'll have to. . . We'll have to break a window. What would my old dad say, if he could see me smashing windows in my own school? Still, it's in a good cause. . ."

He smashed the nearest window with the head of his broom, then used the handle to knock away the last few shards that clung around the edges of the window frame, sharp and spiky as a shark's dentures. When the way was clear he clambered awkwardly inside, and Buster hopped in after him.

The kitchen seemed to be deserted, but Buster still felt nervous. "Empty!" grumbled Mr Creaber, peering inside a huge store-cupboard.

"And this is locked!" complained Buster, tugging as hard as he could at the handle of a king-sized fridge. "Who'd bother locking a fridge?"

The caretaker made a hissy noise between his teeth. "There's something very wrong here, all right. . ."

As he turned away, scratching his head, the fridge door suddenly burst open, knocking Buster flying. A gingham-clad shape sprang out.

"Mr Creaber!" Buster yelled. "Watch out!"

The caretaker turned just in time to duck as Poppy the dinner lady swung her king-size ladle at his head. He recovered quickly, parrying the blow with his broom, and soon a fierce broom-against-ladle fight broke out, sending pots and pans clattering to the floor. "Come on, Mr Creaber!" Buster yelled, as Poppy slashed wildly with her ladle and the caretaker tried to bip her in the belly with the business end of his broom. Buster snatched up a big frying pan from the draining board and started forward to help, then whirled round, sensing a movement behind him. Miss Burtle was stepping out of the fridge! She closed the door and stood with her back to it, fumbling for something in the pocket of her apron.

"Mr Creaber!" shouted Buster.

Behind him, the fight stopped. Mr Creaber and Poppy were both looking at the head dinner lady. The caretaker looked as surprised as Buster to see her standing there – Poppy just seemed to be waiting for instructions.

"I thought you said that fridge was locked?" panted the caretaker.

"It *was*!" Buster said.

"Wilfred Creaber!" sniffed Miss Burtle. "What are you doing here?"

"I just came to find out what you're up to in my school canteen, Beryl," puffed Mr Creaber, still out of breath after his battle. "Or should I say . . . *Myrtle!*"

Buster turned back to watch Miss Burtle, wondering how she would react. She just laughed.

"So you've finally worked it out, have you, you old fool? Yes, I *am* Myrtle Burtle. My stupid twin sister had no idea how much money could be made from this dinner-ladying racket! It was almost my duty to get rid of her and take her place!"

"What have you done with my little Beryl, you. . ." shouted Mr Creaber, but Myrtle Burtle had found what she had been groping in her pocket for; it was a little black handset, like the remote control for a TV or a video, but with only one button – a big, red one, right in the middle. As Buster watched, wondering what it would do, she pressed the button. Behind him he heard a sort of "Sklonk! Waoooooooooooh! Splat!" noise. When he looked round, there was no trace left of Mr Creaber; only his broom clattering on the tiled floor and Poppy grinning evilly.

"So, Mr Bayliss," growled Myrtle Burtle, "we meet again!"

"Here! What have you done with Mr Creaber?" demanded Buster.

"Oh, you won't be seeing him again," she said, and glanced at Poppy. "Get him!"

The muscle-bound dinner lady lunged at Buster, but just in time he managed to swing his frying pan up. It hit Poppy in the face with a noise that was much more musical than anything the School Orchestra had ever produced – a sort of echoey *Dingggggggggg!* in the key of C. "Oooogfhh!" grunted the dinner lady, flailing backwards and knocking a big pile of pots and pans off the kitchen table with a deafening xylophone jangle.

"Don't let him escape!" shouted Myrtle Burtle again, but Buster was already escaping. He jumped up on to a work surface and threw himself headfirst out of the window that Mr Creaber had smashed earlier, landing on the tarmac outside with a blazer-mangling thud. "Help!" he shouted, but he knew there was not much chance of anybody hearing: the only people within earshot were the School Orchestra, and from the strangled farts and bellows that were blatting out of the music room it sounded as if they had just reached a really loud bit of their tuba concerto.

The door of the kitchen crashed open, and Myrtle Burtle came sprinting out, waving one of those holey, plungery things you use for mashing potatoes. "Urp!" said Buster, stumbling up and starting to run. Nobody was going to mash him! But as he rounded the end of the canteen he met Poppy tumbling out of the main door, looking as if her close encounter with Buster's frying pan had done nothing at all to improve her temper. "Eep!" squeaked Buster, ducking a nasty swipe from her ladle. He changed direction, heading back the way he had come, and zigzagged wildly as Myrtle Burtle lunged at him with her masher. He got past her, but as he ran on he could hear both dinner ladies pounding along close behind.

There was nowhere to go but into the narrow gap between the canteen and the playground wall where the wheelie bins lived. He ran to the end and started to climb up on to one of them, hoping that from the top he would be able to jump on to the wall and escape. But the bin shifted under him, throwing him down on to the ground. "Aargh!" he groaned, noticing another big rip in his shirt and wondering what Mum would say.

The big bin, heavy with unwanted scraps of dinner, trundled away from him and crashed against its neighbours, which also started moving, quickly gathering speed. When Miss Burtle and Poppy came round the corner of the canteen, expecting to find Buster cowering trapped and helpless in the alley, they were met by the sight of three bins trundling towards them like overweight Daleks. They tried to scramble out of the way, but Poppy wasn't fast enough and Myrtle Burtle tripped over her. They landed in a heap, and Buster heard a thud as the first bin crashed into them, followed by some clangs and a splattery, splobby sound as the other bins collided with the first one and fell over, spilling their cargoes of smelly scraps. "Aaargh!" roared Myrtle Burtle. "Euuurgh! My beautiful flowery apron! Ruined! You idiot! Get off me! Grab that boy!"

6
CUSTARD YOU CAN TRUST

Buster wasn't hanging about to be grabbed. He hurdled the struggling mound of garbage and dinner ladies and went sprinting across the playground to the school gate. He ran along Crisp Street, sprinted down Dancers Road, cut through Poskitt Parkway and hared up Piecroft Villas. He didn't stop until he was quite sure there were no dinner ladies behind him. Then he flopped down on a bench beside a bus stop and dug about in his rucksack until he found a biscuit he'd been saving for just this sort of emergency*. It had got a bit melted down there among the lost pencils and forgotten PE shorts, but he managed to peel most of the foil wrapper off and soon the restorative powers of chocolate were

---

*It was one of those really nice chocolate ones with the gooey minty stuff inside, biscuit fans.

helping him to recover from his fright and think about what to do next.

He tugged his tattered blazer off and stuffed it inside his rucksack so that Mum wouldn't see the holes when he got home. Then he trudged back to Dancers Road and found a telephone box. He dialled 999. "Please, Police!" he told the switchboard operator when she asked which service he wanted. "I mean, Police, please!" And when the police picked up the phone he blurted, "My school's being taken over by an evil dinner lady only she isn't a real dinner lady she's her evil twin and they've kidnapped Neville and I think they might have eaten him and Mr Creaber went to sort them out but Myrtle Burtle pressed this remote control thingy and he sort of vanished!"

"Oh dearie, dearie me," said the policeman on the other end of the phone. "That sounds very worrying."

"They're probably trying to take over the world," said Buster helpfully. "That's what usually happens. I'd try and stop them myself, but I'm *always* having to save the world and, I mean, that's *your* job, isn't it, so I thought I'd phone you."

"Hmm," said the policeman. "Would you like

us to call out the army and the air force and MI5?"

"That ought to do the trick," said Buster. "As long as they bring some helicopters and really big guns."

"Well, you're out of luck, sonny," said the policeman. "You're from Crisp Street School, aren't you? We just had a call from your head dinner lady to warn us that a nasty little prankster called B. Bayliss was going to phone us up and tell us stupid stories about her."

"Argh!" groaned Buster. "But that's her! That's Myrtle Burtle! It's all part of her cunning plan!"

"Yes, she said you'd say that," the policeman said.

"But she's evil!"

"Hmmm," said the policeman. "Now who should I believe? A very nice and sensible-sounding dinner lady who promised to provide free cakes for the next Policemen's Ball, and complimented me on my rich and manly telephone manner, or a snotty little kid who goes around making up fibs about his elders and betters? It's a tricky choice. . ."

"I'm not snotty!" protested Buster. "At least, I might not be – you can't possibly tell over the telephone. And it's not a fib!" But the policeman had already hung up, and the line was dead.

"Bother!" Buster said. He used his last 20p to call Polly's house. Orchestra practice must be over, and Fake Auntie Pauline would have picked Polly up in that enormous four-wheel-drive car of hers, which could crush Minis under its ginormous tyres and shoulder buses out of its way, so he was pretty certain she would be back home by now. Buster knew she would want to hear what had happened while she had been busy making appalling noises in the music room, but when he asked for her, Fake Auntie Pauline said sniffily, "She can't come to the phone, Buster."

"Why not?" Buster gulped. "Don't tell me the evil dinner ladies have got her too?"

"Evil dinner ladies? Whatever are you babbling about, you peculiar child? Polly has only just got in from orchestra practice. She's very tired, and she's got a big day tomorrow, so I want her to rest quietly and not have to listen to a lot of silly rubbish from the likes of you, Buster Bayliss."

And she slammed the phone down, in the manner popularized by members of the Smogley Constabulary.

* * *

Buster stomped home, grumbling to himself about grown-ups and how impossible it was to make them see what was right under their noses, like dinner ladies' evil twins trying to do who-knows-what in the school canteen. Poor old Mr Creaber had probably been fed into the sausage machine by now, and not even the grumpiest of grumpy caretakers deserved that. He would have to remember to tell Ben and Tundi to steer clear of the canteen sausages for a week or two. . .

His last hope was that Mum would believe him and know what to do, but when he plodged into the kitchen and dumped his rucksack he saw at once that she wasn't in the mood to hear about evil twins and vanishing caretakers. She was staring at him with a sort of questioning frown, which involved one eyebrow going all curly and up while the other squidged right down behind her specs. "Well, Buster," she said crossly, "what's all this about Parents' Evening?"

Buster thought fast, and came up with a Brilliant Ruse.

"What Parents' Evening's that?" he asked innocently.

"You know perfectly well what Parents' Evening!" Mum snapped. "I've just had your Fake Auntie Pauline on the phone, asking me if I'd like a lift to the school tomorrow night. Can you imagine what a twit I felt? Why didn't you let me know there was a Parents' Evening coming up? Is there something you don't want your teachers to tell me?"

Buster's brain flickered like a video on fast rewind, showing him some of the things that had happened at school that term: a sorry parade of missed homework, water-bombs, cheeky answers, running-in-the-corridor incidents and feather-filled tubas. "No," he said weakly. "It's just. . . It's just. . . It's just that the School Orchestra are playing, and I thought that after last time you wouldn't want to go anywhere near!"

Buster's mum gave a sort of shudder, and grabbed the kitchen table for support. It was true that she had heard the School Orchestra's rendition of "O Little Town of Bethlehem" at the Christmas concert, and people who had been through something like that didn't easily forget it. Even so, she was determined not to miss this Parents' Evening. She knew what Fake Auntie Pauline would say if she didn't go – "Aha! So Erica's afraid to find out what Buster's teachers really think of him!" Of course she *was* afraid to hear what Buster's teachers really thought of him, but she didn't want Fake Auntie Pauline knowing that.

"Now, listen to me, Buster Bayliss," she said.

"You're going to come straight home after school tomorrow, and get into your best clothes, and comb your hair, and we're going to go to Parents' Evening together like a proper mother and son."

"Awwww! Mum! Not the hair! Anything but that!"

"Not another word," warned his mum, "or I'll make you wear a tie as well. A pink one."

Buster didn't think she'd really dare do anything so cruel, but he didn't want to push his luck too far, so he said nothing, just plodged meekly into the living room and flumped down on the sofa. He wondered if this would be a good time to mention the goings-on in the canteen and the fact that he couldn't go to school tomorrow for fear that Miss Burtle's evil twin would turn him into school dinners, but from the way Mum was making tea* he could tell that she was still cross and probably wouldn't listen to a word he said. She would probably be *glad* if he got turned into school dinners!

He put the telly on, hoping it would help him to forget his worries. Unfortunately it was summer time, so there was an international swimming competition on instead of *Lumpy-Headed Aliens* and golf instead of *Pop Bucket*. The third

*Very loudly.

channel he hopped to was showing a horrible girly Australian soap opera with KISSING. Euuuuuuuuurgh! He quickly hopped to the fourth, and was rewarded with a helicopter's eye view of the outskirts of Smogmouth. There was a large, smouldering hole in the middle of the industrial estate, and all the houses around it were yellow.

"This was the scene in downtown Smogmouth today," the announcer's voice announced, "after the exploding custard menace struck at the CustCo factory in Toad Road. Britain's remaining custard factories have all been closed down as a precaution, and anyone with any tins of custard in their larder is advised to contact the authorities immediately and await the arrival of the custard disposal squad.

"However there is some good news. Dishy Damon Crumble, TV's Flying Chef, has identified a new brand of non-exploding custard which he believes may end our national custard crisis."

Damon Crumble appeared, wearing a T-shirt so jazzy that it made the TV picture fizz and crackle. He was holding a tin with a red and yellow label, and beaming happily. "That's right, Trixie," he said. "The Ministry of Afters has been testing out all the different brands of custard at a top-secret custard-testing range on Salisbury Plain, right, and so far every single one has proved to be highly dangerous and explosive. Heavy! But I've personally discovered one really monster new brand which isn't just perfectly safe, it's, like, really really tasty! It's made by this company called Scoffco, right, and they promise to have their custard in all the supermarkets by the beginning of next week. Kickin'!"

Buster couldn't believe his ears. Had that stupid chef really said "Scoffco"? He leaned closer and closer to the TV screen until his nose was pressed against the glass and static electricity made his hair stand on end, but he couldn't quite make out the name on the tin in Damon Crumble's hand. Then he jerked backwards with a yelp as the picture suddenly changed and an enormous dancing tin of custard seemed to spring out of the screen at him.

"*Scoffco Custard is the best!*" the tin sang. "*Tastier than all the rest. Scoffco Custard, it comes in a can, and it never, ever goes off bang!*"

"Why not treat yourself to SCOFFCO CUSTARD this weekend?" asked a silky-smooth voice. "Scoffco – It's Custard You Can Trust!"

Buster changed the channel; swimming might

be boring, but it was a lot less confusing than the news, and he was already quite confused enough. If Scoffco was a custard-making company, why did they want to run school canteens as well? And why was Scoffco custard immune to the exploderizing plague? Buster's brain wasn't really equipped to answer difficult questions like that*. He thought about it until a smell of over-cooked brain cells started wafting out of his ears, but he couldn't make sense of it at all. Evil twins, custard, dinner ladies and TV chefs shimmied around inside his head but refused to settle down into a nice, understandable pattern. He wished he was dealing with something nice and simple, like ravenous alien sprouts or marauding monster socks.

There was only one thing for it. He would have to ask Polly. She was brainy enough to work out what was happening. The trouble was, he couldn't phone her, or Fake Auntie Pauline would tell him off again. He was going to have to go to school tomorrow after all!

* * *

Night fell, and darkness swirled into Ashtree Close like a double helping of canteen gravy. Something moved stealthily along the street. Dull grey

---

*The only questions Buster was really any good at answering were the ones that went something along the lines of, "Would you like a chocolate biscuit?"

metal glinted between the parked cars. Rubber-tyred wheels squeaked, *squik, squik, squik.*

Pansy brought the hostess trolley to a halt outside Buster's house, and used high-powered binoculars to peer in through the chink in the living-room curtains at Buster's mum, who was reading an archaeology book, and Buster, who was dressed in his Godzilla jim-jams and drinking cocoa.

The evil dinner lady suppressed a chuckle and drew out a mobile phone with a customized gingham-pattern casing. "Miss Burtle? The boy's at home. Everything seems normal. Doesn't look as if he's told anyone. You want me to grab him?"

"Not yet," hissed Myrtle Burtle's voice out of the tiny hand-set. "We don't want to attract any more attention than we have to. We'll deal with Buster at school tomorrow. He must not be allowed to interfere with my plans!"

7
CAPTIVES OF THE CUSTARD CUPBOARD

Buster set off to school next morning well prepared. In the pocket of his trousers he carried his trusty catapult, and a selection of pebbles that he could ping at the shins of any dinner lady rash enough to try and kidnap him. He was alert and on-edge as he started off along Ashtree Close, darting from the shelter of one lamppost to the next and scanning the gardens and bushes ahead for any sign of gingham-clad assailants. But he soon got bored with that, and was relieved when he bumped into Ben and Tundi on the corner of Dancers Road. He walked the rest of the way to school with them, discussing computer games and arguing about whether *BloodBucket 3* was better than *Doom Cupboard of the Vampire Gutmanglers.*

He completely failed to notice Poppy peering at him through a newspaper with two eye-holes cut in it from the shelter of the Crisp Street bus stop, or the gingham periscope which popped up through a drain cover to track him as he crossed the playground.

That morning in class . . . nothing happened. At least, Buster was vaguely aware that some history and maths was going on somewhere nearby, but it didn't affect him. At breaktime he kept a nervous eye on the canteen, but the dinner ladies stayed safely inside, hidden behind their steamed-up windows. He found some of Polly's friends, but Polly wasn't with them — they told him she was in the music room, going over plans for the concert with Miss Taylor. Buster ran off to play Busterball. "Tell Polly to be sure and wait for me in the *Confidential* office at lunch!" he shouted as he zoomed away. "I've got something really important to tell her!" (He didn't spot the gingham-swathed arm which poked out of a manhole, pointing a high-powered microphone at him to record every word he said.)

After break, there was some geography (or it might have been French). As soon as the lunch-bell rang, Buster whooshed out of his classroom at something only just under the speed of light and sprinted up the stairs. He ran past the NO RUNNING sign outside the staff room and got up enough speed to skid the rest of the way down the corridor to Miss Brown's door. Polly was at her desk, making angry corrections to a rude crossword that some boys from 3a had submitted for the school magazine. "Honestly!" she said crossly. "Seven across – *nickers*. Four down – *big wobbly botom.* They haven't even spelled it right! I don't know what Crisp Street is coming to!"

"That's nothing!" said Buster excitably. "Have you seen Mr Creaber this morning?"

Polly looked puzzled. "No. . ."

"Nor has anyone else, 'cos he's not here. I asked Miss Ellis, and she said he's been called away to visit a sick friend, but everybody knows caretakers don't have any friends, and besides, I saw what really happened to him. . ."

He quickly sketched in the details of what had happened yesterday after school, while Polly's eyes grew wider and wider behind her glasses until he started to worry that they might fall out. When he had finished his story she said, "You're sure this is true, Buster? You didn't just make it up so I'd forget about your article?"

"Honest!" said Buster.

"Then where did Mr Creaber go?"

"I don't know!" Buster insisted. "I heard a sort of *Sklonk – Waooooooh – Splat!* noise and when I looked round he'd just vanished. Maybe Myrtle Burtle's remote control thingy dematerialerized him!"

He had expected Polly to tell him off a bit more for failing to get an interview, but instead she just looked worried and rummaged in her weirdly tidy school-bag. "This came this morning," she said, pulling out a postcard and handing it to Buster. It showed a smiling Spudsylvanian cheesemaid superimposed on to a photo of Count Primula's Castle, along with the words, "Greetings from Splött, Capital of Sunny Spudsylvania!" On the back were some cheese-shaped Spudsylvanian stamps and a neat little message: *Dear Polly, Having a lovely time in Spudsylvania. Sorry I left without saying goodbye, but my mum and dad got some last-minute plane tickets. See you next term, Neville.*

Buster's poor confused brain got a little bit more confused, and he had to sit down. "So Neville really is in Spudsylvania?"

"I don't think so," said Polly. "He's never sent me a postcard before. I don't think he even knows my address. I think it's a fake, to trick us into *thinking* he's OK. I phoned his house this morning, and his mum and dad are still there – *they* think Neville got a last-minute place on a school geography trip to Smogmoor. They'd even had a postcard from him there. But he can hardly be on Smogmoor *and* in Spudsylvania, can he?"

"Then you believe me?" asked Buster, relieved. "Those dinner ladies really are up to something?"

Polly nodded. "The question is, what?"

Neither of them knew the answer, and as they sat staring at each other the door opened and Miss Brown came in, looking all flushed and excited. "Buster! Polly! I've just been talking to Miss Burtle. She says she's very sorry for the misunderstanding about Neville's camera the other day, and as a way of saying sorry she'd like to treat you both to a slap-up dinner in the canteen!"

Buster and Polly jumped out of their seats with shouts of "Agh!" and "Eek!"

"I knew you'd be pleased," Miss Brown laughed.

"But we can't!" blurted Polly. "We mustn't! It's a trap – I mean, we've already eaten our packed lunches. . . I mean, we were about to," she added, remembering that her own lunchbox was open on the desk beside her, still full of the sandwich she had been about to eat when Buster burst in.

"Well, I'm sure you can manage a little more," said Miss Brown sweetly. "Miss Burtle promises ice cream for afters, and chocolate roly-poly!"

"But. . ." Polly stammered, trying desperately to think of more excuses, "but I've got to play in the concert for Parents' Evening tonight!"

"Well, you'll need a nice big lunch inside you, won't you?" said Miss Brown.

Buster realized that there was nothing for it but to tell the truth. "She isn't Miss Burtle!" he shouted. "She's Miss Burtle's evil twin, Myrtle Burtle, and she's kidnapped Neville and Mr Creaber and she's probably making them into sausages right now!"

Miss Brown laughed prettily. "I think some-body's been letting his imagination run away with him, don't you, Polly?" She steered the two children out through the classroom door, and there in the corridor stood Poppy and Petunia, waiting for them. Poppy looked a bit battered and bruised, and a faint smell of wheelie bins rose from her uniform, but she smiled sweetly when she saw Buster.

"Thanks a bunch, Miss Brown!" grinned Petunia, reaching out to grab Polly's arm in an enormous, hairy fist.

"Yes, we'll take it from here," rumbled Poppy, taking a good firm grip on Buster's collar before he could make a run for it. "Nice one, Miss Brown!"

"That's all right!" trilled Miss Brown. "Enjoy your lunch, children!"

"But. . ." said Buster and Polly, as the dinner ladies started marching them swiftly away towards the canteen. They looked back hopelessly at Miss Brown, but she just waved and smiled. *Honestly,* thought Buster, *grown-ups!* He thought about his catapult, which he could feel nestling uncomfortably in his trouser pocket, but he didn't see how it could help him now; Poppy and Petunia would see what he was doing before he could even fit a pebble to the elastic.

"What are you going to do with us?" he asked, as Poppy shoved him out through a side door into the playground.

"That's for the boss to decide," growled Poppy, scratching her stubbly chin with her free hand. "You two have been asking a lot too many questions: she's decided it's time to shut you up."

"But I've got to play my tuba at eight o'clock!" wailed Polly. "If I'm not there for the concert, James MacCallum from 3a will have to do my bits, and he's terrible!"

"What, worse than you?" asked Buster, incredulously.

"Shut up, Buster!"

"Yeah," agreed Poppy, "shut up!" And she clamped a big, beefy hand over Buster's mouth.

"Mffgafffrrbblfgg!" Buster shouted, hoping to attract his friends' attention as the dinner ladies hurried towards the canteen, but everyone else in the playground was so busy playing marbles, zooming about like jet fighters, duffing each other up or resting their brains after a hard morning's schoolwork that they paid no attention to Poppy and Petunia or their prisoners. Chuckling evilly, the dastardly dinner ladies dragged their captives in through the kitchen door. Poppy hauled open the huge store cupboard, and Polly and Buster were thrust inside. As the door locked behind them they heard Petunia's voice growl, "You can wait there until we finish dishing up!"

It was dark in the cupboard. The only sounds were two sets of teeth chattering. Buster realized that the door and walls must be very thick, because they seemed to block out all the noise from the canteen and playground. There was probably not much point in shouting for help. "Help!" he shouted, just to check.

"Ow!" said Polly, in the dark beside him. "What's the point of that?"

"Just wanted to see if anyone could hear," said Buster.

"Well, I did. It was right in my ear. Stop it!"

"Sorry," said Buster. He got out his catapult and tried pinging a biggish pebble at the bit of the darkness where he thought the door was hiding.

"Ow!" yelled Polly. "Now what are you doing?"

"I thought I could smash the lock with my catapult."

"Well, that wasn't the lock, that was me. Ow!"

"Sorry."

They were quiet for a bit. Then Polly said, "Do you think there's any way out of here?"

Buster tried to sound brave. "Course there is. Those dinner ladies are only grown-ups. We'll outwit them easily."

Polly grumbled something about a certain person not having enough brains to outwit a dead earwig, but Buster ignored her and started feeling along the walls for a light switch. They were unusual walls; covered in sort of rounded metallic humps which grated against each other with tinny noises as his hands groped over them. Something fell past him and landed with a thud.

"Ow!" screeched Polly. "That was my toe!"

"Just looking for a light," said Buster.

"Well, what about this dangly cord thing that keeps hitting me in the face?" asked Polly. "Do you think that could be a light switch?"

"Pull it and see."

There was a click, and they were both dazzled by the sudden blurt of light from a naked bulb on the ceiling above them. As soon as he could see again, Buster ran to the door and crouched by the lock. In stories, daring schoolboy detectives are always getting out of villains' lairs by picking the locks of their cells with a humble hairpin. Even weedy girly ones with names like Julian seem to manage it, so Buster didn't think he'd have much trouble. But this lock looked a lot more complicated than he had expected. It was huge and shiny and not at all the sort of lock you expected to find on a kitchen cupboard. It looked more like something on a high-tech bank vault in a heist movie. Also, Buster realized, with a sort of sinking feeling, he didn't *have* a humble hairpin.

"Er, Buster," said Polly, in a tiny, nervous voice.

Buster turned, and gasped. The walls that had felt so strange in the darkness were not really walls at all. The cupboard was nearly full, and he and

Polly were standing in a small open space at the edge of an enormous, shadowy mountain of tins. He didn't need to read the red and yellow labels to know what was in them. "Scoffco custard!"

"But the canteen doesn't serve custard any more!" said Polly.

"Maybe they're going to start again."

"But why is there so much of it? If everybody in the school had custard for their first course and their afters every single day it would still take them about twenty years to eat all this lot!"

"I don't know. . ." Buster sat down on a pile of tins and scratched his head. "It doesn't make sense. When Mr Creaber was looking round in here yesterday he opened this cupboard, and I heard him say it was empty."

"They must have had a delivery this morning," suggested Polly.

"But why just custard?"

"Maybe it was a mistake. Mummy did that once when she went shopping on the internet. She tried to order ten pots of yoghurt, but she left her finger on the 0 button a bit too long, and we ended up with 10,000,000,000 pots. You wouldn't believe how sick we all got of yoghurt after the first few months. . ."

Buster shook his head. He was remembering

what he had seen last night — Miss Burtle and her accomplices loading crates into that lorry. Could it be custard that they were smuggling off the school premises? What if these tins hadn't been delivered here at all? What if this was where Scoffco custard came from, and this was a fresh batch, waiting to be loaded into another lorry, after school today, and driven off to shops and supermarkets?

But why would Scoffco use Crisp Street School canteen to cook up their non-exploding custard? Surely it would be a lot easier just to make it at a factory, where you didn't keep getting distracted by having to dish up dinners for a lot of obnoxious children. . .

"Urrrgg. . ." said Buster, feeling his brain start to go wobbly at the edges with the effort of so much thinking.

The lock clacked, and the door opened. This was good news, because it stopped Buster's brain from melting and trickling out of his ears and making a mess of his school uniform. But it was bad news too, because standing in the open doorway were Miss Burtle and her three burly hench-ladies.

Buster drew his catapult, but Miss Burtle lunged forward and snatched it from him, slipping it into a pocket of her apron. "Lunch-hour's over!" she said, with a sinister smile. "Now it's time to deal with our special guests!"

Buster and Polly cowered against the wall of cans. "Would you like us to wash up?" said Polly hopefully.

"Polly!" shouted Buster, angry at her for putting ideas into their captor's head. He had seen the huge pile of dirty trays and dishes stacked up beside the sink, and he thought almost anything would be better than having to wash them up. Then he remembered what had happened to Neville and Mr Creaber and changed his mind. "Good idea! I'll dry!"

"I don't want you to wash up," said Miss Burtle, still smiling. "I want us all to have a nice cosy little chat. Look, I've even made a plate of chocolate cookies."

Buster poked his head out of the cupboard to see where she was pointing. On the edge of a nearby work-table perched a plate of the biggest, chocolatiest chocolate cookies he had ever seen. Interesting rumbly noises came from beneath his blazer, reminding him that he had been kidnapped on an empty stomach. "Cor!" he said.

"Buster!" said Polly, grabbing him by the back of his trousers as he started towards the enticing cookies. "Don't be so silly! They're probably poisoned!"

"Poisoned?" cried Miss Burtle. "Not at all! Show them, Petunia."

Petunia picked up a cookie and popped it into her mouth. "Ooh. Yum! Thanks, boss!"

"That's not fair!" chorused Poppy and Pansy. "We want one too!"

Buster made a huge effort and forced his way out of the cupboard, dragging Polly after him. If all the dinner ladies started scoffing cookies there'd soon be none left for him! He fought his way towards the table, with Polly still protesting and clinging to his trousers, and the dinner ladies scattered out of his way as he reached for the nearest cookie. Behind him, Miss Burtle laughed cruelly.

Buster looked round. "What's so funny?"

"This," said Miss Burtle. From the pocket of her apron she pulled her remote control. She pressed the red button. There was a *Sklonk!* noise, and the bit of floor that Polly and Buster were standing on suddenly decided not to be there any more. "Waaooooooh!" they yelled, dropping through the hole. Buster managed to grab the edge and hung there helplessly, with Polly dangling from his trousers. *A hidden trapdoor!* he

thought. *So this is what happened to Mr Creaber!* He just wished there had been an easier way of finding out.

"Let go!" snapped Miss Burtle, glaring down at him. "Stop hanging about, boy!"

Buster looked down past Polly's frightened face. He saw a dark shaft yawning beneath him, and something thick and yellowish swirling stickily at the bottom. An abandoned cookie dropped past him and fell down and down, vanishing with a sticky plop.

"Custard?!" wailed Buster.

"Scoffco custard, to be precise," chuckled Miss Burtle. "If the lumps don't get you, you'll drown in the runny bits."

"But, but, but. . ." said Buster, desperately trying to keep a grip on the tiles at the edge of the hole. Part of him was thinking that it was kind of cool to go to a school with secret trapdoors and an under-floor custard tank. All the other parts were just very, very scared.

"My mum'll be really cross about this!" he warned.

"And mine!" came Polly's anxious voice from below. "She's expecting to see me play my tuba at Parents' Evening tonight!"

"Shut up, the pair of you!" hissed Myrtle Burtle,

and squidged some of Buster's fingers under the toe of her crocodile-skin shoe.

"Yow!" wailed Buster, letting go with one hand. "Yip!" squeaked Polly, as the waistband of Buster's trousers started to give way.

"'Ere, boss," said Pansy.

"What?" asked Myrtle Burtle, turning to glare at her.

"Maybe we shouldn't drown 'em in custard? Maybe they'd be more use to us downstairs, like the others? We've got a lot of custard to shift."

"That's a good point about their mums, too," said Poppy, scoffing a cookie. "We ought to make 'em write postcards first."

Myrtle Burtle made a disappointed face. "I suppose you're right," she admitted. "Very well. Haul them out. Quickly!"

The three dinner ladies almost fell down the hole themselves in their hurry to pull Buster and Polly free.

"Phew!" muttered Buster – but had he phewed too soon? For now Petunia was holding him under one arm like a sack of school spuds, and with Polly clamped under the other arm she was stomping towards the big fridge-freezer in the far corner of the kitchen where Poppy and Miss

Burtle had been hiding last night. Were they about to be fridged to death?

But when Myrtle Burtle darted ahead to heave the door open, Buster saw that this was no ordinary fridge. There were no shelves, no ice-box, no vegetable-crisper, no forgotten chunks of cheddar growing blue fur; it was just a big, empty, metal box. It wasn't even very cold, as he found out when Petunia dumped him and Polly inside and stepped in behind them, along with Myrtle Burtle. Myrtle swung the door shut and pressed a button on the metal wall, and the fridge gave a sort of shudder. For a moment Buster felt as if his tummy had decided to leave him and embark on a solo career. He recognized that feeling – this wasn't a fridge at all! It was a lift, and it was going down a long way, very fast.

"If I'm not home for tea my mum will be really cross," Buster warned, but the demonic dinner ladies didn't even bother to reply.

"This is all your fault!" grumbled Polly. "If you'd just been able to resist those cookies we might have been able to escape."

"But they were chocolate!" protested Buster. "You mustn't resist chocolate. It's a very important food-group. . ."

At last the plummeting cupboard came to a

halt and the door popped open. Miss Burtle stepped briskly out, and Petunia pushed Buster and Polly after her into a huge chamber which appeared to have been blasted out of the solid bedrock deep beneath Crisp Street. It was softly lit, thickly carpeted, dappled with the shadows of pot-plants, and one wall was filled by an enormous map of Great Britain, dotted with little red lights. The opposite wall was made of glass, and something yellow churned lumpily behind it. Buster realized that he was looking at a side-view of the underground custard tank.

"That's just the smallest of my custard storage tanks!" cackled Myrtle Burtle. "I made a little window so that I could admire all that lovely yellow gloopiness, and watch the fun when an uninvited visitor drops in!"

Poor Mr Creaber, thought Buster, imagining what it would be like to drown in school custard.

"Buster!" hissed Polly, tugging at his sleeve. "Those lights on the map – I think they mark the locations of all those custard factories that have been exploding!"

"Very clever, Miss Hodge," said Myrtle Burtle. She hung up her apron on a black coat-stand and settled herself into a huge, black swivel chair at the head of a long, black table. "In fact, you're a very clever girl altogether, aren't you? A bit *too* clever. There is far too much at stake for me to let you and your silly friends run about asking questions and taking photographs. That's why I've decided to keep you all safely out of the way. Here, fill these in."

She handed them each a Biro and a postcard of Sunny Spudsylvania, exactly like the one Polly had received from Neville Spooner that morning. "Your mums will be surprised when you don't turn up at Parents' Evening tonight – but imagine how happy they'll be when I explain that Scoffco has sent you both on an all-expenses-paid trip to see the famous Spudsylvanian cheese factories! And tomorrow these lovely postcards will arrive at your homes, telling them what a wonderful time you're having! Now GET WRITING!"

Myrtle Burtle could be extremely scary when she wanted to, and Buster decided there was no point trying to argue. He quickly wrote: *Dear Mum, Having a lovelly time in suny Spudesylviania, whish you were her, love Buster XXX.* "She'll never fall for this," he said, handing it back. "I mean, she might believe it for a day or two, but what will happen when I don't come home?"

Myrtle Burtle made a sad face. "Alas," she said,

"there's going to be a tragic accident at one of those cheese factories. Your parents will get a letter from Scoffco next week, telling them that you both accidentally stumbled into some machinery and got turned into cheese straws. It'll be a terrible blow for them, poor dears, but we'll offer them a lifetime's supply of free custard as compensation. They'll never guess that you're really down here under Crisp Street School, working for me!"

"Doing what?" asked Polly angrily. "What is it you're up to down here, Miss Burtle? Are you running some sort of illegal custard factory?"

"A custard factory?" Myrtle Burtle began to chuckle, then to laugh maniacally. "Perhaps you aren't quite as clever as I thought, Polly! Do you think I'd go to all the trouble and expense of taking over your school canteen if I just wanted to build a custard factory? I could build a custard factory anywhere. No, what I have down here is something much more valuable. . ."

She pressed a button on the arm-rest of her big black chair. Steel shutters at the far end of the chamber slid open, allowing Buster and Polly a dizzying view into an even bigger chamber, a vast, shadowy cavern where dinner ladies in gingham hard-hats hurried to and fro on metal walkways or drove about in little electric buggies, towing trailers stacked high with tins of Scoffco custard. Down on the cavern floor a broad lake shone yellow.

"Impressive, eh?" laughed Myrtle Burtle madly. "Welcome to your new home, my dears – the world's biggest custard mine!"

8
MINE, MINE, ALL MINE!

"A custard mine?" said Polly. She and Buster went trotting after Myrtle Burtle as she walked out through the open shutters into the echoing hugeness of the custard-cavern. "But that's just silly!"

"On the contrary, my dear Miss Hodge," the fiendish dinner lady purred, "it's very, very serious indeed! Remember, the nation has been rocked to its foundations by the recent spate of mysterious custard explosions. People are too scared to buy the big brands any more. CustCo, Custardcorp, I Can't Believe It's Not Custard – soon they will all be forced out of business, and I, Myrtle Burtle, will be the only custard supplier in the nation! Just think of the prices I'll be able to charge for my guaranteed non-exploding custard! I'm going to be rich! RICH!" Her insane cackles echoed among the stalactites on the roof.

Buster peered past her, down into the depths of the cavern, where floodlights on tall stands illuminated the lake of custard nestling in a hollow of the rock. He could see people tramping to and fro down there, scooping up bucketfuls of the yellow glop and emptying them into a big vat.

"Not many people at Crisp Street realize that the canteen custard is actually a mineral," admitted Myrtle Burtle, taking a firm grip on the collars of her captives and shoving them ahead of her down a long metal stairway. "That's why it never tastes quite like the custard you buy in the shops, or make at home. But it's near enough. Imagine how I felt when my stupid sister let on that Crisp Street School is built above one of the largest natural custard deposits in the world? The silly sausage had no idea of the money she could make! And it was almost too easy to get her out of the way and take her place. I set up Scoffco, kidnapped all the old dinner ladies and replaced them with some of my own people. Then it was just a simple matter of sabotaging a few custard factories and starting a national panic. Having a son who's TV's famous flying chef helped no end!"

"Gasp!" said Buster, who was getting a bit tired of gasping and thought it might be easier to just say it for a change. "So you're Damon Crumble's mum? No wonder he keeps telling everybody about your custard!"

A loud, mechanical hooting sound drowned out his words. BEEP, BEEP, BEEP, VEHICLE REVERSING. . . Buster and Polly stuck their fingers in their ears and looked towards the source of the din. Out of a circular tunnel which opened off the cavern a huge, caterpillar-tracked machine was backing, driven by two dinner ladies. As it edged out into the glow from the lamps around the custard-lake, Buster saw that its long, gleaming nose was an enormous drill, designed for biting through rock. "Wow!" he said.

"That's my boring machine," Myrtle Burtle explained.

"Oh. It looks quite interesting to me."

"Idiot child! I don't mean 'boring' as in 'dull', I mean 'boring' as in 'boring a vast network of tunnels through the solid bedrock beneath Smogley, to open up rich new custard-seams'. It's also allowed me to link this cavern to the other school canteens that Scoffco runs, so that we can use them as distribution points for the custard we mine. . ."

Buster remembered the strange noises he had heard echoing up through the floor of Mr Creaber's office. He would have quite liked to hang around and have a look at the massive machine, but Myrtle Burtle dragged him briskly past. They were nearing the custard lake now, and a heady, custardy whiff filled the air, making Buster long for a rhubarb crumble mountain to go with it. The poor custard-miners trooped to and fro in their custard-splattered clothes, lugging their brimming buckets, while grim-faced dinner ladies armed with egg-whisks and meat-tenderizers looked on.

"The best thing about my operation down here," chuckled Myrtle Burtle, "is that it's all free! The custard just wells up out of the earth, and I'm gathering quite a little army of workers who scoop it up for me and don't get paid a penny. Now grab a bucket, and get to work!"

Buster found a heavy zinc bucket thrust into each hand, and an egg-whisk prodded him on the bottom, shoving him towards the custard lake. Following the other slaves, he went out along a narrow metal jetty, dipped his buckets

into the warm, gloppy yellowness, heaved them up full and started the long trudge back towards the custard vat. He couldn't believe his bad luck. This must be the most boring job in the world! It was even worse than tidying his bedroom!* And he was probably stuck down here for ever!

Polly marched past him with her empty buckets on the way to the lake and said, "Don't worry, Buster, she can't make us work too hard, there are all sorts of rules about tea-breaks and holiday entitlements. . ." but somehow Buster didn't think Myrtle Burtle would pay much heed to rules like those.

He up-ended his buckets over the waiting vat and the custard splattered out with a flubbery noise. He was just turning back towards the lake when he realized that there was something very familiar about the two small, scruffy custard-miners staggering ahead of him, clinging to king-size custard buckets. Something very, *very* familiar.

"Harvey?" he hissed. "Cole?"

The Quirke Brothers looked round at him. "Buster!" said Harvey. "So they got you too?"

"But what are you doing here?" Buster whispered, walking as close behind his friends as he dared and trying to imagine how they had got

*At least, he imagined it was — he'd never actually tidied his bedroom, so he couldn't know for sure.

mixed up in Myrtle Burtle's deranged plans for world custard domination. The Quirke Brothers didn't even go to Crisp Street School; they were pupils at St Collander's, over on the other side of town.

"It's those new dinner ladies!" complained Cole, in a whiny sort of whisper. "Our school canteen got taken over by this new company called Scoffco, and me and Harvey nipped into the kitchens one lunchtime to see if we could earn some spare pocket money by helping with the washing up. . ."

"It was a sure-fire money-making scheme," sighed Harvey. "We'd even worked out an advertising campaign. *'Dinner ladies – why waste time washing dingy dishes? Put your feet up and let Quirke Brothers Dish-Washering Services do the dirty work for you. . .'*"

"We were going to pile all the dirty plates up on Harvey's go-cart and take them home and let our dog Hogarth lick them clean," explained Cole.

"But the first thing we saw when we went into the kitchen was a big cupboard full of Scoffco non-exploding custard," said Harvey. "And the second thing we saw was a load of big muscle-bound dinner ladies who grabbed us and tied us up and brought us down here in a secret lift. They said we knew too much and mustn't be allowed to tell tales."

"It's not fair!" complained Cole. "We don't know anything, hardly!"

"Oi!" A dinner lady with a bushy ginger beard leaned close to them and whirred her egg-whisk menacingly. "No talking! Get on with yer work!"

The boys hurried on, but as they crept out along the jetty Harvey hissed, "They might let us take a breather soon. We'll talk to you then!"

* * *

Buster had lost count of the number of buckets he had emptied into the bulging custard vat by the time a hooter sounded to announce a break. The vat of custard was wheeled away to be emptied into the huge custard storage tanks which stood around the sides of the cavern. The miners all went wearily to an alcove in the corner of the cavern, where Scoffco had thoughtfully provided them with a few old canteen chairs and a coffee machine that didn't work. As they wiped the dirt and custard from their faces, Buster realized that he knew some of them. There was Mrs Crust, and Doreen, and Nesta, who had been dinner ladies at Crisp Street before

Scoffco took over. The others must be the former dinner ladies from the other canteens which Scoffco ran. And there in the corner, cleaning the custard off his glasses, was Neville Spooner.

"Crikey!" said the fearless boy reporter, popping his glasses back on and peering at Buster through them. "Buster! I didn't know you were down here as well."

"Neville!" shouted Polly, splodging over to where he stood (her shoes were full of custard). "We thought you'd been dropped into the custard tank, like poor Mr Creaber. . . I knew that postcard from Spudsylvania was a red herring! They made us write some too!"

Neville nodded. "They do something like that for everyone they bring down here. It's fiendishly cunning. What a story it would make for the school magazine! *Evil Dinner Ladies' Cavern of Custard Crime!*"

"If only there was some way we could escape, so you could write it," agreed Polly.

"There's no way out of here, ducks," sighed a large, ginghamy figure flopped on the cavern floor nearby. "I've been down here all term, and I've not found one yet. All day long we have to work under the beady eyes of those rotten guards, and at night they lock us up in here, bound hand and foot."

Buster turned to look at her, and gulped, for at first he thought it was Myrtle Burtle herself, come to eavesdrop on their break-time chat. But when he looked a little closer he saw that this dinner lady was slightly plumper, and her eyes hadn't the mad gleam of Myrtle's. It was Beryl Burtle!

"Miss Burtle!" squeaked Polly. "We thought you'd been done in!"

Beryl Burtle shook her head. "Myrtle needed me alive, to show her where the richest seams of custard were," she said. "To think of it, kidnapped and held prisoner by my own sister! I wish I'd never told her about the custard mine."

"So it was you who discovered it?" asked Polly.

"Ooh, no, dearie. The secret has been handed down from head dinner lady to head dinner lady ever since Crisp Street School was first built. Of course, in the old days, you had to climb down into the caves to get the custard. I used to pop down and fill a few big jugs every morning, ready for the lunch hour. It's that rotten Myrtle who's turned it all industrial, putting in lifts and digging new tunnels with that boring machine of hers."

"And to think," sighed one of the dinner ladies

from St Collander's, "she could have been the greatest dinner lady of her generation!"

"Oh, she was a much better cook than me, when we were at Pigbin's Academy together," agreed Beryl. "But there was always a dark side to Myrtle. At first it only showed in little ways, like helping herself to the hundreds and thousands, or making non-regulation school gravy, without any lumps. Then she started experimenting with recipes of her own – brilliant but twisted things, like upside-down upside-down cakes, and chocolate brownies with real Brownies in. Pigbin's couldn't stand for that, of course. They booted her out. That's when Myrtle decided that she'd use her culinary skills for evil rather than good."

"There's nothing worse than a dinner lady gone bad," said Mrs Crust.

"That's all very interesting," said Buster, who was getting bored again, "but how are we going to get out of here? There must be some way! I don't want to spend the rest of my life lugging tubs of custard around."

The prisoners looked blankly at each other. Harvey Quirke said, "I don't see what we can do, Buster. We'd never overpower all those guards."

"But they're only dinner ladies!" Buster objected.

"No, they're not!" said Beryl Burtle. "Haven't you noticed anything odd about them?"

"They're a bit hairy," said Buster.

"And they've got very deep voices," agreed Polly.

"And a lot of muscles," added Neville.

"And tattoos," said Cole.

"That's because they're really a gang of escaped convicts from Smogmoor High Security Prison!" said Beryl Burtle. "Those three who work in the canteen at Crisp Street are the ring-leaders; Nobby Nurk and his brothers Nosher and Knuckles. Myrtle helped them all to escape so that they could join her in her twisted schemes."

"I *knew* there was something strange about them!" Neville gasped.

Buster had been thinking hard. "If somebody could just get to the lift in Myrtle Burtle's office they could use it to go back up to the school and raise the alarm," he said. "It's Parents' Evening tonight, so there'll be all sorts of grown-ups wandering around who you can ask for help."

"Oh, bother!" wailed Polly, checking her watch. "I'd forgotten about Parents' Evening! It's nearly seven o'clock! I'm due on stage with my tuba at eight!"

"But how could anyone get into Myrtle's

office?" Beryl Burtle objected. "It's locked up tighter than a headmaster's wallet, and with all these guards around. . ."

"We could create a diversion!" suggested Buster.

"What, with traffic lights and cones and big yellow signs and things?" asked the Quirke Brothers.

"No, no, no, just hit a guard or something, and then run up to the office while everybody's looking the other way. . ." said Buster. It had sounded quite sensible when it was inside his head, but as the words trooped along his tongue and jumped out into the open air it sounded sillier and sillier. "Well, it was just an *idea*," he mumbled.

A hooter sounded, filling the secret custard mine with a noise not unlike the opening note of Agasplatt's Tuba Concerto. It was the signal for the prisoners to go back to their dreary work, and their gingham-clad guards came hurrying over to make sure they did. For a moment, Buster found himself walking next to Beryl Burtle. She leaned down and whispered, "It's a good idea, Buster! We need to escape soon; from what you and Neville and young Polly say, it sounds as if my sister's getting richer and more powerful by the day. We've got to stop her. If you get a chance, you make a break for that lift! The rest of us will keep the guards distracted!"

"What, *me*?" said Buster helplessly. "I didn't mean *I* should be the one to escape. I was thinking more of you."

"Ooh, I could never outrun the guards with my poor old legs, Buster," said Beryl. "It's a job for someone young and fit."

"Like Neville!" Buster suggested "Or Polly. Or one of the other real dinner ladies. I don't see why it always has to be me who has to do everything!"

"No talking!" hollered a gruff guard.

The old dinner lady winked at Buster as she picked up her buckets and went back to work. "We're all depending on you, Buster Bayliss!"

9
A SOCKFUL OF CUSTARD

"Aaargh! Pants and Double Pants! Why couldn't I keep my big mouth shut?" Buster grumbled, as he tramped down to the lake and back. But the other prisoners kept looking hopefully at him, waiting for him to run off and fetch help, and Polly had started singing a cheery little ditty each time she passed him. It went, "If Buster doesn't get us out of here (boo-be-doo), I'll tell his mum he put feathers in my tuba (tiddley pom)."

"Oh, all right then," muttered Buster.

And he soon found that having a Daring Escape Plan to think about made his journeys to the custard lake and back slightly less boring. He spent most of each trip furtively looking about, trying to make out where all the fake dinner lady guards were posted, and which stairway would take him back to Myrtle Burtle's office. After a few buckets-full he thought he had it all worked out. All he needed now was a weapon. There were still a few pebbles in his pocket, but they weren't much use to him without his catapult. What else did he have about him that would be powerful enough to overcome one of these burly guards?

Socks! he thought suddenly. The last time he'd been underground he had been chased through a sewer by one of his own socks, which had got so smelly that it had sort of come to life. It had all been a bit embarrassing, actually, but it gave Buster an idea.

The next time he emptied his bucket in the vat he paused, pretending to tie up a trailing shoe-lace before he started back to the lake – and while he was about it he secretly slipped his sock off and stuffed it into his pocket. A faint, cheesy smell wafted out, mingling with the odour of the custard, but none of the fake dinner ladies seemed to notice. Back at the lake, stooping to fill his buckets, he filled his sock as well, stuffing custard into it until little yellow rivulets came squeezing out through the hole in the toe. Surely such a potent mixture of custard and foot-pong would be enough to overwhelm even the toughest escaped convict! When there was no more room inside the sock he tied a knot in the top and turned as if to go back to the vat.

At the end of the jetty the biggest and ugliest of the fake dinner ladies stood on an upturned basin, keeping an eye on the prisoners as they trooped past below him. He was armed with one of those automatic tennis-ball serving machines which had been converted to fire deadly canteen dumplings. The name badge on his frock read "I'm Daisy", but he looked tough enough to be another of Nobby Nurk's villainous brothers.

Buster took careful aim, dropped his bucket and began to swing the sock full of custard around his head. *Vwooooosh, vwoooosh, vwooosh, vwoosh*, it went, whirling faster and faster until it was just a sock-coloured blur. A bit of custard squirted out through the hole in the toe, but then a lump lodged there, plugging it.

"Hey!" shouted Daisy, his attention attracted by the swinging sock – but before he could do anything about it, Buster had let go.

"Eek!" gasped Daisy. He fired wildly with his dumpling gun and Buster and the others quickly ducked as rock-hard dumplings whizzed over their heads, some smashing lights, others slamming against the cavern walls like floury meteorites or splodging heavily into the custard lake. None of them hit the sock, which kept on course, whistling through the air towards Daisy's stubbly face like a fake-dinner-lady-seeking missile.

If you've ever walloped a fake dinner lady in the cakehole with a sock full of custard, you'll already know what sort of noise it makes, so you can skip the next couple of lines. If you haven't, you may be interested to learn that it goes something like this:

Fwoosh!

Yargh!

Ker**SPLETTCH!**

Daisy dropped his dumpling gun and fell backwards off his basin, shouting something that sounded a bit like "Arggleblurgglespluttgluggle!" but was probably much ruder. All over the cavern other fake dinner ladies turned to look, saying, "What?" and "Pardon?" They soon realized that Daisy had been socked in the face and came running to his aid. "Oh, poo!" squeaked Buster, and darted across the cavern floor towards the metal stairs that would take him back to Myrtle Burtle's lair and the lift to the school canteen. A posse of guards ran to cut him off, waving salad forks and cake slices, but the other prisoners were all doing their best to help Buster escape: they up-ended their buckets of custard over the fake dinner ladies' heads, then beat deafening tattoos on them with stolen ladles. The guards, taken by surprise, didn't seem nearly as tough as everyone had feared: Myrtle Burtle had assured them that their prisoners were too weedy to cause any trouble, and they were so dismayed by this sudden revolt that some of them threw down their ladles and ran, while the braver ones were quickly defeated by Neville and the Quirke Brothers, who tipped the custard vat over them.

It was all going better than Buster had expected. He slalomed sploshily through the struggling scrum and started up the stairs, while dumplings ricocheted off the handrail to left and right. A fake dinner lady snatched at his shirt-tails and tried to pull him back, but Mrs Crust whacked the villain over the hair-net with an industrial-size spatula, sending him tumbling into the spreading lake of spilled custard on the cavern floor. "Go for it, Buster!" shouted Polly, knocking another guard over with a well-aimed dumpling. "We can take care of this lot!"

Buster waved at her, and ran on up the stairs. The steel shutters at the top were still wide open. He dived through into Myrtle Burtle's lair. . .

And stopped.

Buster's brain wasn't very good at thinking things through, and when it was dreaming up this Daring Escape Plan it hadn't really allowed for the possibility that the devious dinner lady might actually be in her office — it had sort of assumed she would still be wandering around her mine, gloating. But here she was, seated at a long black table with the Flying Chef himself, Damon Crumble. Petunia, Pansy and Poppy were there too (or Nobby, Nosher and Knuckles, as Buster supposed he would have to start calling them — it was all getting very complicated). Some sort of Important Secret Meeting seemed to be in progress, and Damon Crumble was saying, "There's really no need to blow up any more custard factories, Mum. I've already convinced the great British public that Scoffco's custard is the only safe sort. Now you've just got to get out there and sell it to them!"

"No," said Myrtle Burtle, her round face creasing into an evil grin. "The custard explosions must continue. Not just in this country, but all over the world!" She pressed a button on her chair, and the map of Great Britain on the wall behind her revolved to show the whole world, with constellations of little red dots marking the site of key custard factories. "I want you to start smuggling batches of the special exploding custard into all these factories. Soon, when the whole planet is gripped by panic and weak from lack of custard, they will turn to me, the greatest producer of custard on the face of the earth! The entire global custard market will be mine! Mine, I tell you!"

"Myrtle. . ." said Pansy suddenly.

"Silence!" cried the deranged dinner lady, rising from her seat and turning so that the faint glow from the custard tank fell yellowish across her face. "And don't call me Myrtle. That's a silly name for a criminal mastermind of my stature. From this day forth, I wish to be known as . . . CUSTARDFINGER!"

"But *look!*" Pansy insisted, and pointed a grubby finger straight at Buster, who was standing in the open doorway, wondering what to do.

Miss Burtle swung round, and her beady black eyes zeroed in on Buster like the disruptor-turrets of a Zurgoid space-destroyer. "You!" she said.

"Him!" said Poppy and Petunia.

"Who?" said Damon Crumble.

"Ulp!" said Buster.

There was no escape. Myrtle Burtle's minions scrambled out of their seats and started to close in on him. He turned to run, but Myrtle Burtle pressed another button and the steel shutters crashed shut centimetres from his nose. He doubled back, and managed to slip past Damon Crumble as the chef reached out to grab him, but then he found himself trapped behind the coat-stand, his back pressed against the glass wall of the custard tank, a ring of gingham tightening all around him.

Desperately, he groped in the pocket of Myrtle Burtle's apron, which was still hanging on the coatstand. His fingers closed around the familiar, Y-shaped form of his catapult, and the fake dinner ladies twitched backwards as he snatched it out and set a pebble to the elastic. Damon Crumble squeaked in fright and hid behind his mum.

"Stay back!" Buster warned. "I've got a catapult, and I'm not afraid to use it!"

"Don't worry, lads!" chuckled Myrtle Burtle murderously. "We still outnumber him five to one! He can't ping us all!"

"Oh, yeah, good point," mumbled Poppy, Pansy and Petunia, and flexed their bulging biceps, reaching out for Buster.

At the very last instant, Buster had one of his Brilliant Ideas. Instead of loosing his pebble at the fake dinner ladies he turned and fired straight at the custard tank. There was a loud bang as the pebble hit the thick glass, but it made only the tiniest of cracks, and he had no time to grab another. Maybe it hadn't been such a Brilliant Idea after all. The mocking laughter of Pansy, Poppy and Petunia rang in his ears like a dinner bell as he turned back to face them.

"Now *get him!*" ordered Myrtle Burtle.

"Yeah, grab him!" shouted Damon, peeking over her shoulder.

But Buster could hear a chinking, crinkling, creaking sound going on behind him. It wasn't very loud, but little noises like that can be quite distracting when you're trying to concentrate on getting mangled by maniac dinner ladies. He looked round to see what was making it, and noticed that the tiny crack in the custard tank was widening, turning into a network of wiggly black lines which reached out this way and that across the glass until they looked like a diagram of veins in a biology book. The glass bulged forward under the weight of hundreds of tons of curdled custard. "*Warning,*" said a calm, computery voice from hidden speakers in the ceiling, "*Custard Leak Imminent. Breach of number seven custard storage tank will occur in 0.5 seconds. Run away! Run away!*"

"Oooh!" gasped all the dinner ladies. "You little—"

Just in time, Buster dived between their legs and scrambled into Myrtle Burtle's chair, swinging it round so that the high black back was between him and the custard tank. Then the world went yellow.

"Arrrrrrrrghleglubsplubbbble!" wailed Pansy, Poppy and Petunia, knocked off their feet by a thundering cataract of custard. "Mummy!" howled Damon, as the the yellow tide surged over him and Myrtle and splatted them against the far wall of the office, then splurged about like thick flood water, filled with struggling gingham bodies. Buster jumped out of the chair and started wading through the mess towards the lift at the far end of the office, but as he reached for the controls a plump hand rose from the knee-deep swirl of custard and grabbed his wrist.

"You horrible little vandal!" growled Myrtle Burtle, rising from the depths like the Creature From the Yellow Lagoon. Custard dripped and plopped from her as she heaved herself upright, towering over Buster. "A whole tank of custard, ruined! You'll pay for that!"

"Not so fast!" cried a familiar, grumpy voice behind her. She turned her head, and Buster saw

a skinny, custard-covered shape scramble up out of the gargling, groaning mass of fallen dinner ladies. "You let that lad go, Myrtle Burtle!"

"Mr Creaber!" gasped Buster. "I thought you'd drowned!"

"Not likely," the caretaker said. "This evil creature dropped me into her custard tank all right, but I managed to survive by clinging to one of the lumps and keeping my nose above the surface. I've been floating about in there all night. Now I'm out, I want revenge!"

Miss Burtle made a squeaky, frightened sound and let go of Buster, backing towards the lift. She could see full well that Mr Creaber meant business, and she knew that the only thing more dangerous than an evil dinner lady is an enraged caretaker. "Damon!" she shouted. "Pansy! Poppy! Petunia! Help me!"

But Damon was busy quivering behind her, and Pansy, Poppy and Petunia were still too dazed by custard to do anything but flail about on the floor and burble. Before they could recover there was a furious pounding at the steel shutters, which slid aside to reveal a ragged, custard-spattered band of cheering children and genuine dinner ladies.

"Buster!" shouted Polly, who was at the front.

"Are you all right? In all the confusion you started downstairs we managed to overpower the other guards! You were brilliant! I'll never be rude about your smelly socks again!"

"We tied the fake dinner ladies up in their own cell and piled custard against the door so they can't escape!" chorused the Quirke Brothers.

"They mean tins of custard," explained Polly patiently. "You can't pile custard on its own; it just goes gloop."

"*Super Schoolkids Save Day in Daring Custard Mine Break-out!*" said Neville Spooner excitedly. "*Crisp Street Kids Are Revolting – Official!*" he added, while the Quirke Brothers did a little victory dance and slipped over in the custard.

"Now it's time to deal with that Myrtle Burtle!" growled Mrs Crust, chucking a dumpling at Petunia as he stumbled to his feet and knocking him down again.

Myrtle Burtle looked wildly around. She knew her plans were in ruins. She pushed Buster aside and sprinted into the lift. "You fools!" she shouted. "You'll never catch me! Come on, Damon!"

"Coming, Mum!" The Flying Chef scrambled up out of the custard-slick and dived into the lift behind her. The door slid shut.

"Don't let them get away!" shouted Polly. Buster ran to pound at the controls, but it was no use; the little light above the door showed that Myrtle Burtle and her son had already reached the safety of the school canteen, and no matter how hard Buster pushed the buttons the lift refused to come back down.

"She must have jammed it somehow at the top!" he said. "Now we're trapped down here!"

"Let me have a look at it, Bayliss," said Mr Creaber, wading forward. He fumbled in his pocket and pulled out a screwdriver and a spanner. "I've spent forty years fixing things at this school. I should be able to tackle a jammed lift."

"Wilfred?" whispered Beryl Burtle. She paused in the middle of tying Petunia up and looked at the caretaker. He was so covered in custard that she hadn't recognized him at first, but she would have known that grumpy, creaky old voice anywhere.

Mr Creaber looked round, and almost dropped his screwdriver when he saw her. "Beryl!"

"Wilfred!"

"Oh, Beryl!"

They lumbered towards each other, and soon Miss Burtle was wrapped in Mr Creaber's soggy embrace. It was just like one of those slow-motion-y romantic bits in a soppy film, but with extra custard.

"I thought that wicked Myrtle had done away with you!" cried Mr Creaber.

"And she told me you'd been drowned in custard!" sniffled Beryl.

"Beryl, will you marry me?" asked the caretaker, in a quivery voice.

"Oh, Wilfred, of course!"

"Ahhhhh!" said Polly and all the dinner ladies happily.

"Euuuugh!" said Buster, Neville and the Quirkes, squirming with embarrassment.

"Look, there's no time for all this!" Polly reminded everybody. Even when covered in custard she was a sensible girl, and she had just wiped enough of her watch clean to see that it was twenty to eight. "We've got to get out of here! We only have twenty minutes to get back to school and save everybody's parents from unspeakable horror!"

"You mean Myrtle Burtle might try and wreak a hideous revenge?" gasped Neville.

"Well, that too, but I was thinking more of James MacCallum's tuba playing."

"All right, all right," grumbled Mr Creaber,

untangling himself from Beryl and wading back to the lift. "Keep your hair on."

Polly and Buster and the others watched, hopping about with impatience, while the caretaker carefully undid all the screws that held the lift controls together, carefully put each screw into his pocket, carefully took the front of the panel off and carefully peered inside.

"If he carries on being this careful we'll all be teenagers by the time he gets it working again!" groaned Buster.

Quirke Brother-ish hands prodded his shoulders. "We've got a good idea, Buster!" said Harvey.

"We could nick that big drilling machine thingy," said Cole.

"We could drill our way up to your school in no time!"

Buster looked down into the cavern, where Scoffco's giant boring machine stood waiting. He felt a bit uncertain. He'd gone along with the Quirke Brothers' good ideas in the past, only to find out when it was too late that they weren't good ideas at all, they were really, really, really stupid ones. But he had to admit that there was something tempting about that shiny great machine. "Are you sure we'd be able to drive it?" he asked.

"Easy Peasy!" scoffed Harvey.

"Easy Peasy Squeezy!" agreed Cole.

"We've got a go-kart, and we know how to drive that. That drill thing's probably pretty similar, except for a few minor differences, like, it's got a huge engine instead of pedals, and it bores through solid rock."

"We'll just go straight up, and we'll soon have you back at your school!"

"In time to stop Myrtle Burtle!" gasped Neville.

"In time to stop James MacCallum!" muttered Polly, checking her watch again.

"All right," agreed Buster. "But don't let Mr Creaber and the others know. . ." Something told him that grown-ups might not like the idea of him and the Quirke Brothers behind the wheel of a giant boring machine. Luckily, Mr Creaber was busy peering into the workings of the lift controls, and the dinner ladies were all crowded round Beryl Burtle, congratulating her on her engagement and asking when the big day would be and what she was planning to wear. The Quirkes, Polly and Neville all tiptoed out of the office and went hurrying towards the boring machine. Buster paused to take off his other sock and fill it full of custard, just in case; then he ran after them.

10
BORING

Meanwhile, somewhere above Buster's head, Fake Auntie Pauline was busy wedging her enormous 4x4 into a parking space. The whole of Crisp Street was full of parents in cars trying to park and parents on foot making their way in through the school gates. Most of them were dragging worried-looking children, and Fake Auntie Pauline and Mrs Bayliss felt a bit odd as they stepped out of the big car alone.

"I do hope Buster and Polly are all right," said Buster's mum. "It seems so strange, them being flown off on an all-expenses-paid trip to Spudsylvania like that without time to say goodbye or pack an overnight bag."

"Well, when Miss Burtle phoned me she said

the children would be provided with everything they need," said Fake Auntie Pauline. "It's a terrible shame, of course – Polly missing the concert and everything. . ." But secretly she breathed a sigh of relief; Polly had been practising Agasplatt's Tuba Concerto for weeks and weeks, and the noises that emerged from her room didn't seem to be getting any more musical. Now that that sensible-sounding Miss Burtle had packed her off to Spudsylvania there was no danger of her making a fool of herself in front of the other parents – and probably the concert would have to be called off anyway, because who could take dear Polly's place? She gave a contented sniff as she led Buster's mum up the school steps, safe in the knowledge that she wouldn't have to listen to any so-called music. "Come along, Erica!" she said. "I'm sure you can't wait to hear what Buster's teachers have to say about him!"

Buster's mum gave a faint groan. It was bad enough having a friend like Pauline Hodge whose daughter was top of everything and cleverest girl in the school. It made it even worse when your own child was . . . well, Buster. *Little terror*, she thought, taking a deep breath and following her friend inside. *I bet he wangled this trip to*

Spudsylvania somehow just to get out of coming here with me tonight. Well, let's hope he's having a nice time. . ."

* * *

Meanwhile, Buster was having a really horrible time. There was only room inside the giant boring machine for a driver and a navigator. It hadn't been designed to carry two Quirke Brothers, a Buster, a Polly and a Fearless Boy Reporter. They kept accidentally elbowing each other in the face and treading on each other's toes, and the portholes were starting to steam up.

"Right!" said Harvey at last. "Got it!" He pulled a lever, and the machine shuddered into reverse, speeding backwards towards the lake of custard.

"Aaaargh!" everybody shouted.

Buster shoved the Quirkes out of the way and tugged on a lever marked "FORWARDS" which they hadn't bothered to read. The machine hissed to a standstill just centimetres from the edge of the custard and began trundling in the right direction, steel nose spinning faster and faster until it was just a blur of light, biting into the rock face ahead. *That's got it started,* Buster thought, feeling sort of impressed at himself for being in charge of something so big and powerful, and trying not to pay any attention to the others, who were all clinging tightly to each other, hiding their eyes and going, "Ooo-err!" *Now, I wonder how you steer?*

The boring machine vanished into the cavern wall, throwing out a mass of crunched-up rock in its wake. It drilled a windy path for itself, like the tunnel a drunken woodworm might make inside your auntie's dresser. As it climbed closer and closer to the surface strange vibrations rippled out through the bedrock of Smogley.

On Dancers Road pedestrians felt the pavements wobble and thought, *Ooh! A freak earth tremor!* – but freak earth tremors were so common in Smogley that they didn't bother panicking.

Outside the leisure centre the letter L dropped off the sign that said "COME FOR A SWIM IN OUR NICE WARM POOL", and the people who had been queuing up for an evening dip all suddenly changed their minds and hurried home.

In the playground of Crisp Street Middle School, zigzag cracks started to open in the tarmac, and the bike shed bulged, sagged, burbled and sank with a horrible groan into a deep pit which suddenly opened in the earth. None of the parents inside the main school building noticed; they were all too busy listening to what the teachers were telling them about their children's horrible behaviour and useless schoolwork.

"Mum! Dad!" hissed Masher Harris, who happened to be peering out of a window at the time. "The bike shed just sank into a big hole!"

"Shut up, Masher!" snapped his mother. "Don't think a stupid story like that is going to distract us from what Miss Ellis just told us! Now what's all this about you superglueing first-years to the ceiling?"

Of course, not all the parents had been hearing bad things about their lovely offspring. When Buster's mum caught up with Fake Auntie Pauline in the corridor outside the school hall she found her beaming broadly. "Polly's done *so* well this term!" Fake Auntie Pauline burbled, before Mrs Bayliss even had time to ask. "She's got so many gold stars that there's now a gold star shortage throughout the Greater Bunchester district!" She put on her most sympathetic smile and laid a comforting hand on Buster's mum's arm. "Now Erica, tell me, how is Buster doing?"

"Oh, um, well, where to start?" said Buster's mum. She had been to see each of Buster's teachers, but when she told them who she was, most of them had just shaken their heads in a sad, despairing sort of way, or started to whimper. Several had muttered darkly about feathers. Mr Jaffajee just screamed and hid under his desk. Somehow, she didn't fancy sharing any of that with Fake Auntie Pauline. She checked her watch. "But we mustn't stand here nattering, Pauline! The School Orchestra will be starting at any moment, and we don't want to be around when that happens!"

Fake Auntie Pauline brushed the idea aside. "Oh, don't worry, they couldn't possibly perform without my little Polly."

Buster's mum frowned. She was sure she'd heard a horrible groan a few minutes ago, and felt a sort of shudder run through the school, and she'd assumed that it must be the orchestra tuning up. She called out to two of Buster's friends who happened to be passing at that moment, carrying trays of orange juice and greyish fairy cakes. "Ben? Tundi? Do you know if the orchestra are performing tonight?"

"Yes, Buster's mum!" said Ben brightly. "They're doing something called Arglebarg's Tuna Concerto. It's really horrible!"

Fake Auntie Pauline frowned. "You must have

got it wrong, you stupid boy. How can they perform without my little Polly?"

"Oh," said Tundi, "James MacCallum is going to be doing the tuba bits."

"James MacCallum?" gasped both women, turning pale.

"That's right!" said Tundi. "Fancy a greyish fairy cake? We made them ourselves."

Mrs Bayliss and Fake Auntie Pauline reached out with trembling hands to take their cakes, and Ben and Tundi moved on down the corridor.

"James MacCallum!" whispered Fake Auntie Pauline. "Polly's told me about him! He's terrible!"

"They're *all* terrible!" Buster's mum whispered back. "Come on Pauline, let's get out of this place!"

But as they started to push their way through the throng of parents and pupils towards the exits they saw Mr Fossilthwaite ahead of them shutting the doors. "Ladies and gentlemen," he announced firmly, "will you please take your seats in the hall? The Crisp Street School Orchestra is about to begin its recital. . ."

Fake Auntie Pauline clung to her friend for support as the headmaster wandered past, spreading his message of doom along the crowded corridor. "Erica! What are we going to do?"

Buster's mum hid her fairy cake in a fire bucket and thought hard. "We could still make a run for it," she suggested.

"But it would look so *rude* – and I'm on the Parent Teachers Association! Mr Fossilthwaite will expect me to be in the front row, setting an example!"

Buster's mum looked around in desperation and noticed 1b's big collage of the water-cycle pinned to the wall outside the hall. The mountains, rivers and sea were all very cleverly done in silver foil and scrumpled-up tissue paper, but what caught Buster's mum's attention were the cotton-wool clouds. She sidled closer to the collage, pulled off a couple and stuffed them in her ears.

"Erica!" hissed Fake Auntie Pauline. "That's vandalism!"

"Pardon?" said Buster's mum.

"It's probably a crime!"

Buster's mum glanced at her watch. "About two minutes to eight," she said.

Just then a drony, clashy, blurbly, tootly, scrapy, squawky sort of noise came echoing down the corridor. Either a herd of farting dinosaurs was loose in the school, or the orchestra were getting ready to start. With a quick glance over her shoulder to check that nobody was looking, Fake Auntie Pauline snatched a couple of clouds and hurried after Buster's mum into the hall.

* * *

The boring machine shuddered and shook as it ground its way up through the earth. Buster was just starting to wish he had asked somebody else to drive when it suddenly burst out into the open air and evening sunlight came pouring through the portholes. Peeking out, the Quirke Brothers shouted, "We've come up in the middle of the playground!"

"Great!" yelled Buster, but the machine was wobbling in a worrying way, and he wasn't entirely sure how you turned it off.

"What was that crunching noise?" asked Polly nervously.

"I think it was the bike sheds," said Buster, struggling with the controls. "Hold on, I'll park, and we can get out and see where we are. . ." He wrestled with the controls, but the boring machine seemed to have a mind of its own, and before he could stop it it had up-ended itself and dived back down into the tarmac.

"Left a bit!" suggested the Quirke Brothers, hiding their eyes

The machine lurched upwards again and there was another horrible, splintering crash. Xylophones, recorders and pages of sheet music rained past the portholes. "Buster!" shouted Polly. "You've demolished the music room!"

"Sorry. . ."

Already the machine was on its way down again, taking the wreckage of the music room with it into the stony earth. Buster took a firm grip on the controls, trying not to think about what Miss Taylor would say when she found out what had happened. "One last try," he said.

* * *

"Ladies and gentlemen," announced Mr Fossilthwaite, teetering on the front of the stage and blinking nervously at his audience. Behind him the moth-nibbled red velvet curtains bulged and wobbled; there were some clangs and a toot, and a voice hissed, "Watch where you're sticking that trumpet, Sanjay!"

"I'm pleased to present Crisp Street's very own School Orchestra, performing a very, um, interesting piece of music by Wolfram Von Agasplatt," the headmaster went on. He waited for the usual panic-stricken rush for the exits, but the whole audience just sat smiling at him. Mr Fossilthwaite paused, sure that something was wrong, just not sure what. He didn't know that some of the other parents had spotted Buster's mum pinching cotton wool and spread the word. Now the collage in the corridor outside was mostly nude, and if you looked closely at the parents, pupils and teachers in the hall you could see tufts of cloud poking out of every earhole.

"Ah!" said Mr Fossilthwaite, surprised. "Well then, without further ado, allow me to present Miss Brunnhilde Taylor and the School Orchestra!"

He hopped down off the stage, popping his earplugs in, and the audience clapped and cheered as the curtains opened. None of them heard the thundering crashes and odd grinding sounds coming from the playground, and the orchestra were too nervous to pay any attention to them. James MacCallum stepped to the front of the stage, wobbling a bit under the weight of an enormous antique tuba which Miss Taylor had unearthed for him from the depths of the music room.

"Oh, if only Polly were here!" sighed Fake Auntie Pauline.

"Pardon?" said Buster's mum.

Miss Taylor raised her baton, and the glockenspiel players lifted their little rubber-headed hammers. James's sister Katie, who had heard him practising, dropped her trombone and put her hands over her ears. But before the performance could begin, the whole hall started to shake. Some of the players looked nervously at each other.

"What's going on?" a trumpet whispered to a triangle.

"We don't like it!" whimpered the recorders.

"I haven't even started yet!" said James.

"Just ignore it!" snapped Miss Taylor, pointing her baton at the glockenspiels, and the first twiddly tinkle of the tuba concerto rang out across the hall. James MacCallum took a deep breath and blew so hard into the mouthpiece of the tuba that his feet lifted off the stage. Out came an enormous, tuneless bellow that somehow managed to hit every possible note except the right one. Even the other members of the orchestra winced, but the people in the audience didn't seem to notice. They were all staring at the stage itself, which was starting to heave up into the air at one corner.

"Everybody just keep playing!" ordered Miss Taylor, waving her baton frantically.

The tuba tooted like a puzzled elephant as the entire orchestra slid across the heaving stage and fell off the edge, spilling on to the hall floor in a struggling heap, like ants tipped off a picnic-plate. Behind them, a whirling silver drill-bit the size of a church steeple came splintering up through the middle of the stage and gouged a huge hole in the ceiling, showering the audience with powdered plaster.

Miss Taylor fainted, and the parents all clapped politely.

"Well, that's something you don't see every day!" said Buster's mum.

"I didn't realize there would be special effects," said Fake Auntie Pauline.

The boring machine stopped at last, its nose wedged in the ceiling. The doors popped open and out jumped some small, dizzy, custard-stained figures.

"Look!" said Buster's mum, shaking Fake Auntie Pauline by the arm. "It's Buster!"

"Look!" shouted Fake Auntie Pauline, who couldn't hear a word she was saying. "It's Buster! And my little Polly! And they're all covered in custard!"

Up on the stage, Buster had come over a bit shy at finding all these people watching him, and was trying to climb back into the machine. Polly pulled him out again. "Oh no you don't, Buster! You've got to find Myrtle Burtle!"

"Why me?" asked Buster. "Why can't you do it?"

"I have a concert to perform," said Polly primly. "My audience awaits." She reached down into the muddle of dazed musicians beside the stage and pulled out a tuba.

"We'll go with Buster," Neville Spooner and the Quirke Brothers all chorused.

"No, you won't," said Polly, handing them each a set of hammers. "Somebody's got to play the glockenspiels!"

"Well, I'm not going on my own!" Buster said. "It might be dangerous! She can get away for all I care!"

"Tuba," said Polly menacingly. "Feathers. Quilt."

"Oh, all *right*." Polly could be very commanding sometimes, and Buster knew there was no point arguing. He jumped down off the stage and ran along the aisle towards the exit, waving sheepishly at his mum and Fake Auntie Pauline as he passed. As he pushed his way out into the playground he heard Neville, Harvey and Cole begin a tuneless tinkle on the glockenspiels.

11
CUSTARD'S LAST STAND

The playground was silent and deserted in the sunset; only a few tattered sheets of music stirred, blowing this way and that on the evening breeze like tumbleweed in a Wild West movie. Buster pulled the sock out of his pocket. It wasn't technically a sock full of custard any more, since most of the custard had dribbled out and soaked into his trousers, but the heavy, soggy weight in his hand made him feel a little safer as he prowled towards the canteen.

The kitchen door stood wide open. Inside, the fridge was open too, as if Myrtle Burtle and Damon had been in too much of a hurry to bother shutting it behind them when they ran out. There was nobody about. Buster peered into the store cupboard. Empty! So Myrtle had taken her latest batch of custard with her!

He went back out into the playground. Long shadows stretched across the tarmac, and the dazzle of the low sunlight made it hard to see anything at all. He could hear Polly's tuba pooping and mooing away up in the hall, and beneath it another sound, a faint *squik squik squik*; the sort of noise a not-very-well-oiled trolley-wheel might make.

There, hurrying through the shadows, was Myrtle Burtle, pushing a canteen trolley. There was no sign of Damon Crumble. *She's probably left him behind, or done away with him*, thought Buster. That was the trouble with working for super-villains. One mistake or cheeky remark and they blew you up, or dropped you in their piranha-pool. (They were a bit like P.E. teachers that way.) Anyway, whatever had become of Damon, it was pretty obvious what his mum was up to. Her getaway trolley was speeding towards the school gates, and teetering on its top was a tower of custard tins.

"Stop!" shouted Buster, starting to run after the absconding dinner lady.

Myrtle Burtle looked back and laughed. "Bye bye, Buster! These are the last few tins of non-exploding Scoffco custard in the world, and I'll make enough money selling them to start up a whole new criminal empire!" She clambered aboard the trolley and pulled a cord somewhere near the back. An engine spluttered into life, and a white fist of exhaust smoke punched up into the evening air as the trolley began to gather speed, veering away from Buster towards the school gates.

"Bother!" shouted Buster. He ran after the trolley as fast as he could, out through the gates on to Crisp Street, but it was pulling quickly away from him. He had just one hope of stopping it. He drew out his catapult. He balled up his custard-sodden sock and placed it squelchily in the cradle. He pulled back the elastic with all his might and – *Plinge!* But as the sock hurtled away from him like a tiny custard comet he realized that he might have used a bit too much might: it was arcing right over Myrtle's head and curving down towards the pavement ahead of her. *On the head! On the head!* urged Buster, praying that the airborne footwear would hear him and alter course, but it overshot and landed with a heavy *splodge* a couple of metres in front of the trolley.

"Ha ha!" shouted Myrtle, looking over her

shoulder and waving. "You'll never catch me, Bayliss! Better concentrate on getting your stupid friends out of my custard mine – because I've set it to self-destruct! You can tell your chum Mr Creaber that the whole place will blow up in five minutes! Ha ha ha ha ha! Whoops! Whaaaaargh!"

Busy gloating, Myrtle had forgotten to watch where she was going, and the trolley's offside front wheel had rolled right over the sock. It burst with a splattery splurge of custard and the trolley skidded, slithered, wobbled and went crashing down, scattering evil genius and tins of custard all over Crisp Street.

"Oh, *knickers!*" shrieked Myrtle Burtle.

"Result!" yelled Buster, doing a special victory dance and falling over. But as he scrambled up the sky above him suddenly filled with dazzling lights and loud noises of the thwump-thwump-thwump variety.

"Oh, what now?" he groaned, looking up.

Low over his head a helicopter came clattering, the down-draught from its rotor-blades restyling his custard-soaked hair and rolling tins of custard into the gutters. The doors and windows of nearby houses opened as people leaned out to complain about all the noise, and stared up open-mouthed instead at the huge black

machine swooping at chimney-pot-height along their street. Dogs barked, cats ran for cover, and Buster really, really wished he was at home watching telly instead, because the underside of the helicopter was emblazoned with a big picture of Damon Crumble's grinning face and some day-glo orange letters spelling out, THE FLYING CHEF!

So that's where Damon had crumbled off to! He hadn't been abandoned at all! He'd just gone to fetch his helicopter!

The blast from the rotors squidged Buster flat against the door of Fake Auntie Pauline's car, and there was nothing he could do but watch as a long rope ladder came jiggling down from the hovering helicopter's door. Myrtle Burtle grabbed the bottom rung and started climbing, pausing just once to look back at Buster and blow a loud raspberry. "You haven't seen the last of me, Buster Bayliss!" she promised. "The world will hear from me again!" Then Damon reached out of the 'copter's cabin and grabbed her hand, and the last Buster saw of her was her stockinged legs flailing as she was dragged inside. The ladder was pulled up after her, and the helicopter bobbed, turned and went racketing away across the rooftops.

Buster peeled himself free of Fake Auntie Pauline's off-side passenger door, leaving behind a sticky yellow imprint of himself. He wasn't used to having evil geniuses outwit him and get away scot free. It wasn't right! It wasn't fair! He wandered back into the playground looking as dazed and vacant as an actor in a *Harry Potter* film. Through the open windows of the school hall he could hear Polly's tuba solo was coming to a blurping, hooting climax amid lots of frantic glockenspiel-bonging. It wasn't exactly Wolfram Von Agasplatt's Tuba Concerto in G Flat, but it seemed to have gone down pretty well with the audience – Buster could hear them clapping and cheering.

Weird, he thought. He turned towards the canteen, and was pleased to see that Mr Creaber had got the lift working at last. He and Beryl Burtle stood arm-in-arm outside the kitchen door, admiring the last streaks of sunset in the western sky, while Mrs Crust and the other former captives chivvied the grumbling fake dinner ladies out into the twilit playground. Nesta was using the canteen phone to call the police. Buster watched it all with a faint, worried feeling – he was sure that there was something important he was supposed to be telling somebody, but he couldn't remember what. Something Myrtle Burtle had said. . . Something about how she'd set her custard mine to do something-or-other. . .

"Bayliss!" shouted Mr Creaber, catching sight of him and waving. "You made it!" He hurried over, reaching out to tousle Buster's custardy hair with an even more custardy hand. "Did you see anything of that Myrtle?"

"Er, she got away," Buster admitted.

"Oh, well," said the caretaker. "Not to worry."

"But she said the world would hear from her again! Damon took her away in a helicopter!"

"Nesta's just been telling the police all about that young man!" Beryl announced. "I think it'll be a very long time before he's allowed to present another helicopter-related TV cookery programme. And as for Myrtle's other partners in crime, they'll soon be safely in custardy. Hee hee hee!"

As the real dinner ladies all creased up laughing at Beryl's rubbish joke, Mr Creaber led Buster aside. "You know, Bayliss," he said, "I used to think you were nothing but trouble, but you've done a pretty good job these last couple of days. You've saved Crisp Street School!"

Just then, the floodlights at the school entrance came on, ready for all the parents who would soon be coming out to their cars, and Mr Creaber saw for the first time the state of his precious playground. It looked as if a million maniac moles had been playing tag in it. Even where the Boring Machine hadn't made actual holes there were long hummocks of cracked and shattered tarmac, or worrying dips where it was starting to subside into the tunnels below. The bike sheds had vanished, the music room had been reduced to a sad little heap of rubble with a few mangled instruments sticking out of it, and the climbing frame was tilting like the leaning tower of Pisa.

"Flamin' Ada!" gasped Mr Creaber.

For some reason, the sight of all that destruction jogged Buster's memory. "Oh, yes!" he said. "Myrtle Burtle gave me a message; she said to tell you that she's set her custard mine to blow up in. . ."

There was a huge boom. The whole playground shook, the school bell tower fell off, and every car alarm in Smogley started to cheep. When Mr Creaber looked round he couldn't help noticing that the canteen had collapsed into an enormous hole. Up out of the depths squirted a thick yellow geyser of custard, and the caretaker watched in horror as it splattered across his ruined playground, his school, and his little house at the edge of the playing fields.

"*Buster Bayliss!*" he shouted.

* * *

But Buster always knew when it was time to make himself scarce. He had already slipped quietly away, mingling with the crowd who were pouring out of the school. He heard people saying things like, "I've never enjoyed a School Orchestra concert so much!" and "They're a lot better when you can't hear anything!" and "Pardon?"

Buster elbowed his way through the crowd until he found Neville and the Quirkes. "What happened?' they asked. "Did you get Myrtle?"

"Well, she sort of escaped a bit," Buster confessed. "But all the others are going to be in custardy for a very long time, ha ha ha!"

"You'll have to give me an exclusive interview!" said Neville. "*How I Collared Crackpot Cook! Hero of 2b Tells All!* The next issue of *Crisp Street Confidential* is going to be the most excitingest ever!"

"I'm sorry you got lumbered playing glockenspiel for Polly. . ." Buster said.

"That's OK!" said Neville.

"We enjoyed it!" said Cole.

Harvey opened his jacket to reveal a purloined glockenspiel, and Buster suddenly understood why his friends were all looking so flat and rectangular and gave off little tinkling noises when people bumped into them. "Thanks to Polly, we've realized our true talent!" Harvey explained. "You should have heard that audience cheer! We're not meant to be dish-washer-uppers! We're talented free-form modern jazz musicians, us. We're going to start a cool jazz glockenspiel trio and sell a million trillion billion records. . ."

Buster shook his head in deep bewilderment as the three of them went tinkling off. Then he noticed Mum coming down the school steps, tugging something white and fluffy out of her ears. "Buster!" she said as he ran over to her. "There you are! Well done! But I thought you were in Spudsylvania? I had a phone call from your head dinner lady. . ."

"Must have been some sort of mix-up," said Buster. "I'm sorry I didn't get home in time for tea. . ."

"That's all right," said Mum. "I didn't realize you were involved in that pageant, or performance, or whatever it was. Congratulations! It must have taken ages to prepare! My favourite bit was where you climbed out of that big drilly thing. That was really impressive. It's wonderful what you can do with cardboard and tinfoil, isn't it? Gosh! I'm sure the playground wasn't this messy when we came in. . ."

"No, er, can we go now, please?" asked Buster, glancing quickly over his shoulder for any sign of incoming ballistic caretakers as he dragged her past the wreckage and out into Crisp Street. All he saw was a lot of policemen bundling the fake dinner ladies into waiting cars and saying, "We're taking you into custardy, ho ho ho!"

"It's an absolute disgrace!" announced Fake Auntie Pauline, steaming past with Polly and her tuba in tow. "I've just been talking to Mr Fossilthwaite. Apparently, while Polly was holding us all spellbound with her marvellous tuba improvisation there was a major custard explosion in the canteen! Fancy Scoffco keeping explosive custard on school premises! As a member of the PTA, I'm going to insist that they're dismissed, and the old dinner ladies are brought back!"

While Mum and Fake Auntie Pauline discussed the bad news, Buster glanced nervously at Polly. "Er, Polly, are you sure there's no danger of you mentioning anything to our mums about tuba-ish, feathery sorts of things?"

But Polly was still beaming happily, glowing with the success of her performance. "It's all right, Buster," she said happily. "You should have seen that audience! Usually when I play my tuba people sort of fidget – you know, make silly faces, or hide under chairs, or try to climb out of the window; it can be very distracting. But not tonight! They were spellbound! They just sat there smiling, with a faraway look in their eyes! That was the high-point of my career, and it was all thanks to you!"

Buster had a horrible feeling that she was going to try to hug him – here! Where people might see! – but luckily Fake Auntie Pauline dragged her away just in time. "Come along, Polly; we'd better get back and work out a good, rigorous home-study programme for you; we mustn't have you falling behind in these dreadful extra-long holidays."

She stormed away towards her car, and Polly glanced back at Buster and gave a happy little wave as she was carried along in her mum's slipstream.

"What did she mean about extra-long holidays?" asked Buster, baffled.

Mum sighed. "Apparently the exploding custard caused so much damage that they've decided to close the school until next term so they can get on with the repair work."

"Awooghabargargleboogleurp!" said Buster, a bit over-excitedly. It wasn't his fault; inside his head, his brain cells were all doing the hokey-cokey and organizing conga-lines and celebratory firework displays, which made it a bit difficult to talk. Extra-long school holidays! No more lessons until next term! That was almost a whole lifetime away! And Mr Creaber was sure to have forgotten his little accident with the boring machine by then.

"No school for AGES!" he yelled, dancing in circles around Mum as she walked out of the school gates. "BRILLIANT!"

"Fantastic," agreed Mum, wearily pulling two bits of cotton wool from her pocket.

"You're going to have the pleasure of my company all day long, for weeks and weeks! Can Ben come to stay, and Tundi, and Neville, and the Quirke Brothers, and. . ."

But Mum was too busy stuffing her ears with clouds to answer him.

"This is going to be the best holiday **EVER!**" shouted Buster.

"About twenty-five to nine," said Mum, and hand in hand they ambled homewards through the custard-flavoured dusk.

PHILIP REEVE

Look out for
more books in this
brilliant series!

Night of the Living Veg

It's bad enough that Buster's mum has dumped
him on her best friend for the week – but it's *just plain
inconsiderate* to make him save the entire town from
invasion by a breed of alien super-cabbage as well.
Especially when he's already suffering torture by
flowery guest bedroom. But he's going to have to do
something to rescue Fake Auntie Pauline – even though
anyone who attempts to feed him leek-and-tuna-fish-
bake deserves to get eaten by a sprout-monster...

The Big Freeze

Why does the world always have to end right
in the middle of the summer holidays? Buster is not
happy – Smogley is suddenly full of bossy trees,
rampaging ice-monsters and fairies who are most
definitely armed and dangerous. Something has to
be done – and guess who's going to have to do it?
No one understands that Buster's *busy* – he has
some serious not-going-to-school to do. Honestly,
it just takes one load of crazed ice-beings
to really spoil a good summer...

Day of the Hamster

Buster's mum has made it very clear – Buster
is never, *ever* to bring home any more school pets.
Not after the gerbil. The goldfish. And the ... *stick
insect.* But Buster has been lumbered with Hamish
the Hamster and a whole houseful of hamster-stuff
for the weekend. There's only one possible way out
of this – the Quirke Brothers' new Pet Hotel, where
Hamish will be pampered, petted and certainly
not fed gloopy brown stuff that will turn him
into a hamstersaurus rex...